Dreams of Pelagy

G. A. Borrero

In honor of my mother, a woman who did everything on her own with a heart full of love, and the women like her.

Contents

01 – Diving Deep

News of what the queen Lai-Zemforau had planned spread throughout the palace and seven seas like the contagion they considered mankind to be; no communication was had that did not at least briefly touch on the impending doom awaiting the surface dwellers. When the scuttlebutt had made its way to the Princess, she swam off to the throne room posthaste.

Lining the platform near the furthest-back-most wall was an array of eight thrones – one large one of carved coral, and seven smaller ones of sea glass to its left. The first three smaller thrones each had a male sitting in them.

Upon a large throne sat a woman; she had long, flowing dark midnight-blue hair and icy eyes that pierced the depths. She was bare-chested, and white-blue flesh gave way just below the hips to red scales encased in gold. She found her eyes mirrored in her daughter, except her daughter's eyes hinted at the cold, dark depths of the ocean they called home. The Princess was her near-replica, though the scales she bore were white with gold instead.

"Mother-Queen," spoke this daughter, bending at the waist with her arms out and down. Her multitonous voice reverberated and rippled pleasantly through the water as she spoke. "I formally request an allowance for the humans."

The queen glared out at the younger mermaid. "We cannot allow their insolence to continue to go without punishment, Lai-Kuuvalu. They destroy our seas, our food supplies. They destroy their land, their own food supplies. They murder each other in droves, surely for sport."

Lai-Kuuvalu inhaled the salty water that she knew was

not as pure as it once was. "I seek not grace nor forgiveness for them. If you would allow it, send a representative to land. Have them speak to the leader of the humans. They may yet be reasoned with."

"Did you forget what happened to that pitiful human girl, when we tried to reason with the human Alexandros?"

Lai-Kuuvalu lowered her gaze. She opened her mouth and sang,

> *Take thy Greatness*
> *Child of Man*
> *May our songs give you strength*
>
> *Safe passage, eternity, await you*
> *Child of Man*
> *May our songs elevate your soul*
>
> *The Posidni Elixir will make you beautiful*
> *Child of Man*
> *May our songs chill your core*
>
> *Do not share our gift, or else a curse awaits*
> *Child of Man*
> *May our songs hold you*
>
> *She was not the intended*
> *Child of Man*
> *May our songs torture*
>
> *Now she will wait forever for you*
> *Child of Man*
> *May our songs haunt you*

"Ah, so you do remember. This pleases us," said the queen. "Perhaps our ancestor's mistake was to gift our form as an elixir; we should not have had commune with Alexandros. Likewise, naught but terror awaits our kind and theirs if we try to communicate once more."

Lai-Kuuvalu countered, "And if we do not, you will flood the planet and kill them as far as your waves can reach, Mother-Queen."

"That is of no concern to you, Heiress, unless you intend to involve yourself directly."

"I do." Lai-Kuuvalu straightened her back, arms at her sides.

For a moment, the queen's arm, ventral, and ear fins all flared in a display of emotion. Just as soon as it happened, it was swept away by the current. "We forbid it as your Mother."

"It is my duty as Heiress to approach each situation as calmly and coolly as possible, with a level head," Lai-Kuuvalu said flatly. "I am not asking for permission as your daughter, I am asking for your leave as your Heiress, Mother-Queen."

The queen stared at her daughter for a long time. The water took on a frigid quality as the symbol of Neptune on the Queen's cheek shone a bright cerulean in the darkness... but then the glowing faded. "You may have your leave for a period no longer than one year. You have that time to convince us to change our mind. No Posidni in her right mind would support you or your cause. If you die during that time, no human will be spared, regardless of your cause of death. Do you understand?"

"Yes, Mother-Queen."

"You are to leave now."

Lai-Kuuvalu responded, "Yes, Mother-Queen," with the same steadiness as her first, but the hints of surprise stirred within her chest.

"It is the cold season. Head to the shores of New Jersey. You are less likely to cause a ruckus coming to land there. Do not trust man to keep you safe, Lai-Kuuvalu."

"Yes, Mother-Queen," the princess repeated.

"If it comes to saving your life, use your sonar."

"Yes, Mother-Queen." Her surprise peaked further, but she dared not let it show.

"Take your holo-clam with you. We expect regular reports."

"Yes, Mother-Queen," she repeated a final time, voice reverent.

The glimmer in the Queen's eyes reflected resignation, but her posture remained upright, and her tone held its strength. "Go."

Lai-Kuuvalu dipped into another bow before her mother before turning and swimming out of the throne room, white scales with their golden rims glimmering in the darkness.

"My Queen," said one of the three male mer seated in considerably drabber thrones beside hers. "Are you actually going to humor the Heiress's request?"

The Queen slowly turned and looked at him; a shiver overtook his form. "Whether I do or do not is of no matter to you, male. Know your place."

"... yes, my Queen." All three of the men lowered their heads respectfully.

The Queen looked to where her daughter had been.

She would surely return, ready to sing her tales of the unworthiness of humanity.

02 – Washed Up

Shoreport, New Jersey. Famous for nothing. An unequivocal shithole on the Jersey Shore. Such a shithole, in fact, that the number of tourists was decreasing every year. After that bitch Sandy had made mincemeat of the sandy beaches, nobody wanted to visit. Too many sandbars. It was too dangerous. Even the locals avoided the water and pier. The pier and port that had sunk the city into near-bankruptcy to repair. And it was only nearly so on a technical level; Shoreport was severely in debt.

The school system was among the worst in the state, and that dishonor extended farther to being in the bottom 100 schools in the country. They somehow managed to have a community college, Shoreport Community College or SCC for short, but the basic classes had abysmal standards and the degrees were nothing short of a joke; who in this day and age needed a degree in sailing? There were a handful of associate degrees offered that were actually decent, but the infamy of the school system overshadowed the legitimacy of the knowledge obtained when it came to those few degrees.

Who had inherited this mess other than the current mayor, Feodor Neftali Petrov? He stood on the pier, looking out at the Atlantic that seemed to reach on forever before him, his arms resting on the metal bars to keep people from slipping down to sand a good seven feet down. Some kids liked to slide under the bars anyway, and he knew it would take just one lawsuit from an over-concerned parent of one of those little shits to put the city in financial ruin.

The waves rolled in; the waves rolled out. He sighed and asked aloud, "How did a place with such a great view end up such a fucking mess?" His eyes settled on the horizon. "God, you owe me an explanation, or at the very least a solution. There is no way I can fix this place on my own, and being a mayor has made me surprisingly powerless."

Just then, a large Atlantic breaker made way to the shore. As the foam pulled back, laying in its stead was a pale, curvaceous woman. She was surely as naked as the day she was born, save a strange pearl necklace with a golden clam pendant. Her wavy hair was jet black and clumped together with the brown seaweed found along the shore. She was coughing and heaving.

He caught sight of her and rushed to the stairs to make his way to the beach. Feodor yelled out, "This is neither an explanation or a solution!" He drew closer to the woman and knelt at her side, sand digging into his black slacks. "Hey, hang in there." He started patting her back. The woman coughed and gagged, and spat up cigarette butts and pieces of plastic bag. "Ew..."

"What..." she coughed again. "... what matter of uncleanliness is this, that you keep your waters like this?"

"Listen... you're naked, it's freezing, and clearly, you're not right in the head." Feodor worked on taking off his coat. "Let's bring you to a hospital to get fixed up, maybe get you on your meds. Where did you come from?" The woman was quiet for a too long moment. "Where...?"

"The Royal Palace in the capital," she responded.

"The royal... okay. You're from DC. And you decided, hey, it's December, let me go skinny dipping at the Jersey Shore. Sound about right?"

"No, not at all. Are you mocking me?" she asked briskly. The already cold air had a noticeable temperature drop.

"A bit. Your story is ridiculous," he explained. "What's your name?"

"Lai-Kuuvalu," she responded, coughing up some more garbage. "Ugh..."

"Lai-Kuuvalu... your parents are the real creative sort,

aren't they?"

"What is that supposed to mean?" she asked, glaring at Feodor. Dark brown, almost black, eyes met hers.

Feodor put his hands up defensively. "You are the most apprehensive woman who almost drowned. Are you sure you're from DC and not from New York?"

"I'm from neither place." She moved to sit on her legs, holding his coat to her body. "I need to talk to your leader. It's urgent."

Feodor put on a robotic voice and motioned with his arms as if he was one as well. "Beep boop, take me to your leader." He stopped and looked at her face. "You're completely nuts, aren't you? Where are you from, if not DC or New York? You sure as shit ain't from Jersey."

"I only have a year to convince my mother to not kill your kind, and you're worried whether or not I am food."

"What…" he sighed and moved to sit on the sand, shivering. "Let's try this again. My name is Feodor. What is your name?"

"Lai-Kuuvalu."

"Alright. Lai-Kuuvalu. Where did you come from?"

She opened her mouth and sang a small clip of Posidni language, each set of her vocal cords working in tandem to make an otherworldly, beautiful sound.

"Whoa. Okay. That was… I can't pronounce that. That wasn't a language. What was that?"

"It was a language. It is the language of the Posidni. I told you the name of where I come from."

"Which state or country is that?"

"It's the seas."

"The seas," he repeated dubiously.

"Yes, the seas. That was the name of the capital within the sea your kind calls the Atlantic."

He pinched the bridge of his nose. "... so, you believe you are a mermaid or something."

"A mer... yes, I am a Posidni, but humans call us mermaids, mermen, merfolk. Yes."

"New name: you are now Ariel Fisher, because you sure as shit ain't a mermaid." He stood up and tried to lift her under her arms. "And you are going to the mental hospital, no matter how hot you are, you are touched in the head."

"I am not hot, you are hot, and my head has not been touched and certainly NOT on the inside." She stared at Feodor as he helped her to her feet. She stood, wobbling.

"Can't you stand? Or did you take too much water?... why am I asking you? I'm just going to call 911 and get an ambulance here." He took out his phone from his pocket. "Then they can do intake and–"

She put a hand on his phone and ice spread from her fingertips across the surface of his phone to his own hand.

"WAH!" Feodor just about threw his phone in surprise. It landed neatly in the sand. He stared at Lai-Kuuvalu, a silence between them as the waves crashed in the background.

"My name is Lai-Kuuvalu. I am the Heiress to the throne, and my mother is the Queen of the Seven Seas, blessed be her name, Lai-Zemforau." Her voice had taken on the same quality as her singing as she spoke those lines several times at once, slightly out of sync. "You will help me, Feodor, without me having to display more of my true self."

Long story short, the next thing Feodor knew, he had this strange, gorgeous, practically naked woman in his car as he drove towards his home. He wasn't sure who was going to be less enthused: Carlotta or her cat Santa Claws.

03 – Land Legs

He pulled into his driveway and parked the car. "You are going to sit here until I return with clothing, and then you are going to get changed. And then we are going to go drive to get you a wheelchair since your legs don't seem functional."

"… changed? Clothing?" She raised an eyebrow. "Do you mean you intend me to cover myself like some impure lowlife?"

"No, I intend you to cover yourself like a God-damned normal person if you want me to help you out at all." The glare she gave him made him roll his eyes. "Fine. Yes. Like some impure lowlife, like the rest of us. Being topless is illegal here, and I could have you fined for public indecency seeing as you're a bit more than that."

"I am beautiful, even in this hideous form," she countered.

A rush of red came to Feodor's dark cheeks. "That doesn't matter squat, you still can't prance around naked. Or should I say crawl, since you're useless from the waist down."

"I have never had a pair of legs before today, and that I have to continue to have them after today for any length of time is one of the single most inconvenient occurrences I have ever had the displeasure to experience."

He grumbled to himself, "Stupid well-spoken crazy not-human whatever-she-is." He wasn't sure he believed her on her being a mermaid. None of the stories he had ever heard of mermaids involved ice powers, and she looked perfect…ly mundane, damn it, snap out of it, Feodor! You have Carlotta! Well. Kind of have Carlotta. It wasn't official, but she had moved in, cat and all. He rubbed his head in frustration as he headed inside.

He went and grabbed a pair of Carlotta's underwear from her drawers, and then went into her closet to take one of the many dresses she decided to never wear. "Carlotta!" He called out. "I'm borrowing some shit!" He waited for a quip about crossdressing, but all he got was the judgmental glare of Santa Claws, sitting on her bed. It let out a typical deep meow. "Yeah well fuck you too, Santa Claws." He headed down the stairs and to the living room. No Carlotta. No note. "Weird. She's usually home by now."

He peeled the ice on his phone off of it and prayed it still worked. When he saw it did, he looked through his messages. Nothing from Carlotta, but her Instagram showed her getting wasted with her friends at a club the next town over. "... again? You're going to ask me to pick you up and throw up in my car. You need to stop acting like we're kids," he said to his screen, knowing full-well she couldn't hear him or respond.

He pocketed his phone and went to his car, opening the passenger door. "Here," he said, taking the coat off of her and dumping the panties and dress on her lap. "Clothe yourself." He closed the door and walked to the other side of the car, making sure nobody driving by would see. "Man, what the fuck am I doing. It certainly isn't my job to do this. Take me to your leader... fuck, I can't bring her to the president. Mermaid or not, she has some weird ice powers." He rubbed his brow. "When I got elected, dealing with a magical maniac wasn't included in the job description..." He turned his head to the side. "Hey, are you done in there?"

And then he spotted her. Her skin was nearly blue in its pale color, the unusual hue brought forth by the orange-yellow dress she wore. It clung to her body more than it did Carlotta's, on account of their different body shapes and sizes. Carlotta was smaller, dainty and pretty and wispy. The same could not be said of his mysterious ice-woman. The dip in the dress's neckline left just enough to the imagination that he found himself uncharacteristically salivating. The Hell is wrong with me, Feodor wondered. I saw her naked already and apparently the dress is making me want to see her naked again.

"I have finished putting on the clothing, if that is what you mean."

He approached the car and climbed in. Feodor put her seatbelt on her for her and then his own. He drummed his fingers on the steering wheel and then looked at Lai-Kuuvalu once more. "Are you sure you're a mermaid?"

She stared at him suspiciously. "I know that is what I said; yes, I am a Posidni."

"Posidni. Which is like a gender-neutral form of a mermaid or something."

"It is a loan word, taken from the name of one of our Gods."

"Wait... Poseidon?"

"Yes, that is what the Greeks called Him."

"What the fuck. Are you Greek?"

"I am not Greek, but there are Posidni and miposidni off the coasts of Greece. I am sure there are a large handful that live there illegally."

"... Illegally." He started the car. "What makes it illegal for them to live off the coasts of Greece?"

"You misunderstand; it is illegal for them to live on land." She looked at Feodor as they talked. "That which belongs to the sea belongs to the Queen, and the ancient laws state we are not to interfere with the humans so long as they respect the sea."

"Oh... uh... oops, I guess," he muttered, driving up to a red light.

"Which is why I must speak to your leader," she said, looking at Feodor still. "Or else my mother will kill all the humans."

The light changed. He didn't budge. He slowly, almost mechanically, turned his head towards Lai-Kuuvalu. "I beg your pardon?"

"She is going to flood the planet and kill all the humans unless I convince her otherwise."

His eyes boggled as he stared at this apparent mermaid.

"Your vehicle has ceased its movement."

"I'm a-fucking-ware. Are you joking? Tell me you're joking."

"I am not, which is why I must speak to the leader of humanity."

He began driving again and started laughing. "Haha. Leader of humanity. Hahaha."

"I fail to see the humor in this."

"Haha. We are so screwed, that's the humor! Even if you spoke to the leader of this country, you wouldn't get all of the countries to listen to you! They are more likely to try to nuke the seas if you really are a mermaid and reveal it!"

Her shoulders lifted as she tensed. "Are you telling me to give up? Because I will not give up so easily. Humanity shouldn't be erased."

"If you stay around us long enough, you're going to agree with your mother. I should throw you back in the ocean. Haha. Hahaha."

"That is a shortcut to floating belly-up, Feodor. I would not recommend it. It would be detrimental to your well-being."

"Haha... ha..." he stopped laughing and gulped. "You're going to meet my girlfriend Carlotta at some point."

"Girl... friend?"

"A woman who I am romantically involved with but not bound by law to," he said with a shrug.

"I am of the royal pod; we do not partake in such frivolity. On the whole for Posidni, a woman picks her husbands and may dispose of them as she pleases."

"Husbands... plural?"

"My mother has three."

"And which one is the king?"

"None of them."

"How is he chosen?"

"He is declared the king by the reigning queen, usually within a few years of marriage."

"Well, lady, you are in for one rude wakeup call: up here, it's the guys who are typically in charge. Case and point: this sucker right here is the mayor of this town. You got lucky that I found you."

"I hardly consider being in your company lucky, male."

"Whoa, no-no, I have a name and I've heard you use it. My name is Feodor. Fe-o-dor. It's easy enough to pronounce. Fee, like the money Shoreport owes. Oh, like oh my God, how much money do we owe? And door, like the door that's going to slam me on the ass when I leave my post next election because I am utterly fucked trying to bring this place back to its previous crappy glory. Feodor."

"... Feodor."

"Yes."

"And my name is?"

"Ariel Fisher to any human that asks because there is no fucking way you will be taken seriously if you say Lai-Kuuvalu, and you will be taken less seriously if you show what you are to most people."

"Are mermaids jokes now?" she asked, bewildered.

"More like myths. Like unicorns and fairies."

"But we're real," she disagreed.

"That you are." They pulled into the parking lot of a 24-hour retail-pharmacy store. "You stay here... don't eat anything or talk to anybody, and please, for the love of God, don't ice my car. It's my only mode of transportation without having to spend extra cash on a cab." He parked the car.

When he went into the store, he walked right past the register to the travel section. He took one of the pillows there, shoved his face into it, and screamed as loudly as he could. Feodor couldn't care less about all the stares he got for doing so, especially as he was the mayor. When he felt satisfied, he went and asked a clerk for where the wheelchairs were, purchased the cheapest one, and headed back to his car with it. He exhaled in relief at seeing his car was still in one piece, and that Lai-Kuu-valu hadn't budged.

Once the wheelchair was loaded into the trunk, he got into his car once more. He turned on the car and started again towards his home. "On the one hand, I'm glad I listened to my dad and got a house that's disability-ready, but on the other, why the fuck does it have to be this situation."

"Fate brought us together, Feodor. It would be futile to fight what's meant to be," she said boredly, looking out the window as he drove. "You would not be my first pick, either. I would rather a woman."

"Are you a lesbian?"

"I am not Greek," she reaffirmed, looking at Feodor once more. "Do you have problems with your hearing? Is my English insufficient?"

"My hearing is fine; your English is older than my grandfather. Do you have romantic feelings for women?"

"Whether I do or do not does not matter. Males are the fairer sex and too gentle to be politicians."

"Do I seem fair and gentle to you?" Feodor laughed.

"You do a poor impersonation of a crass woman," Lai-Kuu-valu responded with a shrug. "You are fairly gentle to not seek to kill me, first thing."

He shook his head a little, doing his best to focus on his driving. "It's the humane thing to do. You're thinking and speaking – that means you deserve at least a modicum of respect."

"Humane..." she repeated, going quiet. The rest of the ride was uneventful, but that was sure to change: a blonde woman stood outside of Feodor's house wearing a short black dress, holding a small black purse, smelling strongly of booze.

Feodor mumbled a single word as Carlotta made eye contact with Lai-Kuuvalu, "Fuck."

04 – Instinct

"Who is she, Feodor?" asked Lai-Kuuvalu.

"That would be Carlotta. And I have to break the news to her that you're staying at the house for a while. DO NOT, under any circumstance, DO NOT MENTION that you are a mermaid. Do you understand me?"

"I do not take orders from any save my mother, and I certainly do not take orders from men," she responded sourly, an equally sour glare on her face as she eyed the man beside her.

Feodor messed his own hair with both hands in frustration. "Grr... then... consider it a strongly-worded suggestion! I'm trying to keep you from becoming sashimi!"

"Why would I become–" Her eyes metaphorically lit up. "Ah. I see. I can defend myself, if she is that dangerous."

"NO. No. No, that is not needed." He unbuckled his seatbelt, climbed out of the car, and closed the door behind him.

Carlotta stormed over, standing in front of the hood of the car. "What the fuck, I go partying for a few hours and you go and get a new girl! I thought we were tighter than that! Three years together and you do this shit to me!"

"Okay, so you need to shut the fuck up because we're in public, Carlotta."

"NO! THIS IS THE FIRST AND LAST TIME, FEFE!" And she started to smack him, open-palmed, hitting at his arms and face in her alcohol-fueled rage.

He grabbed Carlotta's head in his hands and growled, "Stop for a fucking minute and listen to me! Hit me later! That woman in the car is staying in the guest bedroom for a while.

She is very important. Very extremely important."

Carlotta glanced at Lai-Kuuvalu, then looked back at Feodor.

"Do you understand me?"

"Why is she hot?" she whined.

"I have no fucking idea why she's hot," he half agreed, half complained. "Her name is Ariel. Can you treat her kindly? Please? She can't even walk."

"I don't like her. She's going to take you from me."

"I don't want to hear that from you, you promised you were going to stop clubbing months ago, and then I caught you out clubbing tonight."

"You were supposed to come home later, you locked the door on me."

"And you're supposed to remember your keys, yet here we are." He let go of Carlotta's face. He unlocked the front door for Carlotta.

As Carlotta headed inside, she said, "You better not let her interfere in our relationship, Fefe."

"Can you not call me Fefe? You know I hate it."

"Don't act so hate-able then! Hmph!" With that, Carlotta headed inside.

"Argh." Feodor headed to the back of the car and opened the trunk, taking out the box with the wheelchair. He unfolded the wheelchair and when he was satisfied everything was as it was meant to be, he brought it near the passenger side of the car and opened the door for Lai-Kuuvalu. "Well, Ariel. You're lucky she didn't realize you're wearing her clothing."

"I don't like her. She's weak-willed, insecure, and whiny."

"Yes, but she's mine." He unbuckled her seatbelt and lifted her into his arms.

Lai-Kuuvalu looked confused. "You own her?"

Feodor shook his head. "She's my girlfriend." He paused for a long moment. "I think." He set Lai-Kuuvalu into the wheelchair and closed the passenger door. He wheeled her into the house. Once there, Carlotta was waiting, arms crossed. "Carlotta, this is Ariel."

"You should stay with someone else," Carlotta said coldly.

"I would if I could," Lai-Kuuvalu responded.

"Ariel, this is Carlotta," Feodor said, voice dropping as he could see this was going to be a hellish arrangement.

"But why, Feodor? Why do we have to house her? Can't you put her in a hotel?"

"She needs help maneuvering about, and she's important, as I've said."

"So she should pay for a caretaker, you're a mayor, not a fucking nurse."

Feodor pinched the bridge of his nose. "Did you really not listen to anything I said prior to–"

"If it's easier," Lai-Kuuvalu offered, face and tone betraying no emotion. "I could tell my mother there's nothing worth saving."

"Nope!" He said in a rushed panic. "No. That won't do. Nn-nn." He looked at Carlotta. "You either get used to her being here or you can move somewhere else for a while."

"This shit is why we're not official yet."

Feodor's face flushed with anger and embarrassment, but he simply responded, "I am not engaging you on this in front of Ariel. You can suck up your insecurity and deal with the situation at hand or you can escort yourself out of the house."

"It's my house, too!" Carlotta said as she stomped a high-heeled foot with a click-clack.

"No, only my name is on the deed. It's my house and solely my house. I wanted it to be your house too, but you said you didn't want to do anything permanent with me."

"Being a human male seems confusing."

In an exasperated voice, he proclaimed, "Ariel, you don't know the half of it!"

"I'm glad I do not have to suffer such inconveniences."

Carlotta observed Lai-Kuuvalu with a great deal of uncertainty. "... she talks weird."

"She *is* weird."

Just then, who came down the stairs but Santa Claws. He padded his way over to Lai-Kuuvalu and jumped on her lap, curling up there and purring.

"Whatever. She can stay, I guess." Carlotta stormed upstairs to her and Feodor's bedroom.

Once she was out of earshot, he asked in a hushed voice, "How did you do that? With Santa Claws."

"Oh, that's simple," deadpanned Lai-Kuuvalu. "Cats like fish."

05 – Drowning on Air

The evening wound down with the three of them having sushi together, delivered to their house from the one Japanese restaurant in town. One pizzeria, one Japanese restaurant, one Chinese restaurant, and one diner: that was the entirety of the eating-out scene of Shoreport. Feodor was grateful Shoreport even had that much; he wasn't sure what he would have done, growing up, if there weren't as many cuisines as there were.

Lai-Kuuvalu looked across the small table at Feodor. "I need to utilize the bath at least once a day, along with all of your salt."

"Of course you do," Feodor sighed heavily. It only made sense.

To him, at least.

"Is that some sort of beauty treatment? Salt water?"

Lai-Kuuvalu opened her mouth to speak, but Feodor spoke over her, "Yeah, Carlotta. And we have to accommodate her because she is so important."

"You never let ME take any salt baths!"

"You never even asked, how am I supposed to allow you to do something you never asked for permission for?" He was pretty sure salt water would eat at the pipes. "No. You know what? New plan. There's that floatation place in Ocean. We'll drive up to Ocean daily and you both can have your salt water."

"That is amenable to me."

"That is... amazing! You're finally spending your money! Oh, Fefe, I knew you had it in you!" Carlotta hugged onto Feodor's arm. He looked less-than-enthused.

"Stop calling me Fefe."

"You know you love it."

"I'm doing this for Ariel, not for you. You're just getting a free ride for the floatation tank on account of the fact if I don't offer it to you as well, you're going to be on my ass for the next year over it."

"Or longer," Carlotta agreed cheerfully.

"... What's with that look, Ariel?" Feodor asked, staring at her now. She was holding her chin, leaning forward, staring at the couple.

"Is this form of courtship typical? I have never seen or heard of anything like it, where I'm from."

Carlotta puffed out her chest as she said, "This is how everybody gets together! It's natural."

Feodor shook his head in disagreement. "It's not natural or typical, it's just how Carlotta and I are." Feodor wormed his arm free from his girlfriend.

"And he loves it this way!"

"I don't, you do."

"I do!"

Lai-Kuuvalu had already finished her sashimi, and the other two were just about done with their food. "Feodor, how do I operate this wheelchair?"

"How pampered *are* you?"

"Carlotta, lay off. Here, let me carry you upstairs."

"When are you going to carry *me* upstairs? You never carry me past the couch!"

With a shrug, Feodor got up and wheeled Lai-Kuuvalu out of the kitchen to the staircase. "Tomorrow at lunch, I'll bring you to... fffuck you'll have to come with me to work. That's fine. I'm a leader, even if I'm not the one you're looking for, we can help each other out. Maybe." He parked the wheelchair next to the staircase and carefully lifted Lai-Kuuvalu into his arms and began to scale the stairs, holding her. He strained with each step.

"Is something wrong, Feodor?"

"You're heavy."

"I am much lighter in the sea."

"Yeah, I bet that's what all mermaids say when they're essentially called fat," he mumbled. His shoulder began to feel cold as she glared at him. He shivered and said, "Oi, cut it out, or else I won't be able to hold you and we'll both go tumbling down the stairs!"

"Yes, and with some luck and timing, you will be beneath me."

Again, warmth overcame Feodor. "That's not how I'd want to experience that," he said.

"There's a way you would prefer?"

"Shh... shut... stop it. You're confusing me. I have Carlotta."

"Of course you do," she said, the light playing off her eyes to make them appear twinkling. "She lets you get away with so much backtalk, it's astounding. I have never seen a more dysfunctional relationship. Are you at least happy? I imagine a male who is allowed to speak to their woman as you do would be pretty pleased with his freedom."

He made it to the top of the stairs and stopped. His voice dropped. "What sort of question is that? Yes, I'm happy. That much is obvious."

"Is it?"

Feodor walked her to a bedroom and sat her down on a bed there, blue comforter pulled back to display the crisp white sheets beneath. "Goodnight, Lai-Kuuvalu. Tomorrow will be a busy day for us."

"Goodnight, Feodor, Lesser Leader of Man."

"Mayor of Shoreport," he corrected with a small, sad laugh.

Her voice softening a smidge, she corrected her previous statement: "Feodor, Mayor of Shoreport."

The walk downstairs seemed longer than normal and he returned to the table Carlotta sat at. He went to eating his food once more.

"Tucked the weird bitch in?"

"… are you ever happy about anything I do?"

"I'm happy when you buy me clothes, or take me out to fancy restaurants," Carlotta said, nearly done with her sushi.

"That's it?" he asked, setting down his chopsticks as he looked at her.

"What else is there?" It was only now that he noticed the caked-on makeup Carlotta took the time to put on every day to hide the wrinkles and other natural imperfections coming through on her face. He thought of the times he had taken her out on dates – she was always deeply involved in the activities, but not the time they had together. They didn't hold hands unless she was taking pictures to show them holding hands. They didn't do things together unless she wanted to show him off or she wanted to try and make someone else jealous… or both.

"Why are we together?"

"Why do you put such weight on the word "together"? We're fuckbuddies, Fefe," Carlotta said with a too-chipper voice. "What else is there?"

The sex was fantastic. He couldn't deny that much. But, even so… "That isn't enough for me anymore."

"Well I'm not going to date you seriously," she said as she returned to eating.

"I wasn't going to ask you to. I think we need time apart."

"Time apart isn't for fuckbuddies, that's for boyfriends and girlfriends," she responded cheerfully. "So it doesn't apply to us."

"Fine. Let me put it more bluntly. This isn't working out anymore."

"I'm fine with us keeping things as they are, minus the sex."

"You still aren't getting it."

"What's there to get? I'm amazing and a catch, you're grateful that I spend any time on you at all, and you're welcome!"

"Carlotta. You have by the end of the week to move out." Feodor got up from his seat and threw out the plastic container his sushi had come in.

"Excuse me?"

"You're excused."

"No, no, no. You can't throw me out. What will I do? Who will take care of me?"

"The next guy who thinks you're amazing and a catch. Or, you could, y'know, go to work, get a job, be responsible for yourself like an adult."

"Is this because of her?" Carlotta got up and held the chest of Feodor's shirt. "Don't let her ruin what we have, we have something great!"

He gently removed her hands from his shirt. "What we have is a lie, a classic case of use and abuse."

Like always, his words were met with an open-handed smack. "How could you!" And then another. "Who do you think you are to treat me this way!"

He grabbed her hands and lowered them down. "Listen here, Carlotta. You hit me again, I will ruin my reputation and yours by calling the cops for physical abuse."

"It'll be my word over yours, and you're a man in a position of power."

"I have Ariel here and she's seen how you've treated me.

Now enough of this." He let go of Carlotta's hands. "You're sleeping on the couch tonight."

"That's where the guy sleeps when there's an argument."

"Not in his own home it's not." He left the room and went to Lai-Kuuvalu's room. She was laying in bed awake. "Do not kill Carlotta."

"If she attacks me, I will react," she said calmly.

"Please do not kill her. I don't want the police at my house."

"I suspect something has transpired?"

"I called it off with her just now."

"You? With her?" For a brief moment, her eyes seemed to show hints of quiet laughter. "She allowed it?"

"Human relationships... well... err... around here, at any rate, only require one person to say it's no longer a relationship. She and I apparently didn't even have a real relationship."

"You will have to explain it to me plainly, Feodor."

"Not tonight... probably not tomorrow either. Thank you for making me understand."

"... thank you for listening."

He regarded her for a long moment and the blue, blue eyes that seemed to shine in the room's darkness with their large pupils. She had a beautiful face, but he knew it was magic. Or maybe it was her biology. He wasn't exactly sure which, but he knew she was a beautiful human by some means other than what humans considered natural. For a moment, Feodor pondered if she looked the same as a mermaid, to which Lai-Kuuvalu responded, "I look very different in my true form."

"You can read minds, too?"

"You were staring up and down my body. Either you were contemplating asking me to join you in your chambers, or you were wondering about my shape. The more likely was the latter."

Feodor tapped his hand on the doorpost twice. "Goodnight again, Lai-Kuuvalu."

"Goodnight once again," she responded. He closed her door and went off to his room. He closed and locked the door to his bedroom, praying that tomorrow he would wake up tomorrow from this strange dream.

But that didn't happen. He woke up early and headed to Lai-Kuuvalu's room. When he opened the door... there she was, sleeping in the bed. He closed the door. He opened it again. She was still there. He tried this a few more times, but each time, there she was, sleeping in bed. He went over to her and placed a hand on her bare arm. Her skin was cool to the touch and... dry. He gently shook her. "Hey. Wake up, Lai-Kuuvalu."

At hearing her name, her eyes snapped open. She quickly flipped to her back and opened her mouth, facing him... and found herself in a stare-off with him. She slowly closed her mouth.

"Good... morning?" he asked unsurely.

"Do not wake me when I am in hostile territory," she warned him. "I could have killed you."

"By opening your mouth?"

"I was going to blast you with sonar."

"S... sonar..." he reaffirmed, color draining from his face.

"Yes. Correct. Sonar."

"Why the fuck are you so dangerous?! Sonar, ice powers, what can't you do!?"

"Fly," she deadpanned.

He smacked his forehead. "Great, the deadly fish has a sense of humor."

"Don't tell my mother." She moved to sit up and rubbed her other arm unsurely. "I will need salt water soon. I am drying out."

"Tap water won't do?"

"Not unless it has salt in it as well."

"So you're a saltwater fish. Are there freshwater mermaids?"

"Posidni," she said.

"Yeah, them."

"There might be, if they were on land sufficiently long enough to get to a lake or river and found one deep enough to feel at home, and if over generations they evolved to handle the water properly. It is easiest for us to breathe saltwater, followed by freshwater, then the atmosphere of our ancestors, and lastly air."

"Atmosphere of your ancestors?"

"I wouldn't wish to bore you with the history of my people, as fascinating as it is," she said, moving to swing her legs over the side of the bed. She placed two unsure feet onto the ground and tried to put weight on them, but they already showed signs of giving way without her even getting off the bed.

"Here, let me carry you." Feodor lifted her into his arms. His back ached from doing this yesterday, and it continued to ache now. "We'll teach you how to walk yet."

"I have no time for such things. I must speak with–"

"I know, I know," he sighed.

Once he got her down the stairs and in the wheelchair, he brought her towards the kitchen and froze, passing the living room. It was in shambles: the flat screen TV had been knocked off the wall, the glass for his china closet had been shattered, his fine china had been broken on the floor individually in one centered spot, his laptop was sitting in a puddle of soda on the ground, and a bottle of his finest wine lay still and empty. On the couch was Carlotta, her hair a mess, her mascara having created runny lines down her cheeks, and a satisfied smile on her resting face.

"Carlotta..." he growled out... and then yelled, "CAR-

LOTTA!"

She startled awake, blond curling tresses bouncing as she sat up in a rush and looked at Feodor. "Good morning, Fefe!"

"Good fucking nothing, what the fuck is wrong with you?! Get the fuck out of my house!"

"Let me get changed first, and then, I'll–"

"OUT! NOW!"

She took her time getting up, grabbed her purse, and went to the foyer to get on her shoes. "I'll be back later."

"Your things will be waiting for you when you come back. Outside. On the concrete." When she left, his eyes went to the hook that held their keys. Both of their keys. "... because you certainly won't be coming back in here again, forgetting your keys like always." He let go of the wheelchair and put his hands together.

"What are you doing?"

"Praying for rain."

06 – Green Renaissance

When he pulled up to the office, he parked his car and looked sideways at Lai-Kuuvalu. "Is there any hope for us?"

The silence between them was filled by the crashing of waves in the far distance and the piercing cry of seagulls overhead.

"I don't know. I'm here because I'd like to think there is," she finally responded, a hint of softness to her voice he was unsure he imagined.

He opened his mouth to speak, but closed it. What was there to say? She canted her head slightly in response to him likely looking like a beached fish. Feodor shook his head and climbed out of the car. "One second, I'll get your wheelchair." He waited for some thank you or an acknowledgement, but all he got was the sound of her unclicking her seatbelt.

With a heave and a pull, Feodor hoisted the wheelchair out of his trunk and set it up. He wheeled it to the passenger side of the car, opened the door, and then lifted Lai-Kuuvalu into the chair. He grunted, "I've said it before, and I'll say it again... You're far heavier than you look, you know."

"Air is the inferior medium; in the sea, I am far lighter and more dazzling."

"Dazzling, huh? You mermaids don't do modesty, do you?"

"I am the Heiress and am an exquisite specimen of my kind, what modesty is needed?" she challenged.

He closed the passenger side door. "I will admit, if the rest of you mermaids—"

"Posidni."

"—Posidni, whatever. If the rest of you Posidni are even half as attractive, humanity's in deep shit. Just come to shore and bat your eyes a bit, people will drown throwing themselves into the ocean just for a chance to get some."

"Get some... what?"

Feodor blushed and groaned. "Oh, come on, you have to know that one!"

"I do not."

"Humans are horny."

Lai-Kuuvalu tilted her head backwards to look at Feodor. "I still do not understand. Humans lack horns, unless they have evolved to have them and it did not make it into our songs?"

"I don't know if I should laugh or cry, haha... hahaha..." Feodor laughed weakly, shoulders trembling. "Let's just shelf that discussion for another time, maybe. Like never. Never sounds good."

Lai-Kuuvalu frowned. "I demand an explanation."

He began to push her wheelchair. "Later," he reaffirmed. He pushed her into the small municipal building. Feodor nodded to the security guard, who was staring on in bewilderment. Feodor stole a peek at Lai-Kuuvalu to see how she was responding to the guard; back straight, shoulders square, head forward with a slight tilt upwards, hands folded neatly on her lap. Her forward-staring gaze was unwavering. *All she's missing is the crown*, he thought.

He took her into a room that was remarkably neat. Sitting at the sole desk was a woman in her mid-to-late 50s wearing half-moon glasses, dark brown skin matched with warm brown eyes and mid-back length box-braids. She wore a lavender turtleneck and had matching lavender nails; she wore a pair of modest black slacks. On each ear was a cowrie shell stud. "Mayor, who is this?"

"Leila, this is Ariel Fisher. Ariel, this is Leila O'Neill, my secretary."

"It's nice to meet you," Leila said as she offered her hand for a handshake, but Lai-Kuuvalu did not extend her hand in return.

Feodor grumbled and said, "Ariel, it's a custom here to shake hands, regardless of rank, when meeting someone new."

Lai-Kuuvalu shot Feodor a look, but then reached out and shook Leila's hand. "Are you new to the West?"

She thought about this for a moment. The West?... is that what they called the land of the Western Atlantic? "Yes," she said uncertainly.

"Well, welcome. I'm sorry you'll be dealing with someone like our mayor. What brings you here?"

"I—"

"Am very busy and I need to take her STRAIGHT to the office, thank you for introducing yourself."

"But what is her..." Before Leila could finish, Feodor had wheeled her off to his office and closed and locked the door.

Lai-Kuuvalu glanced at Feodor. "She is your secretary. She works for you. Why are you frightened of her?"

"That woman is too sharp is why, she would figure out everything if left with you for too long." He wheeled her in front of his desk, and then took a seat at his chair. He took out a note-pad and a pen, looking at her. "… help me help you help us. What do we need to fix?"

"More than you can alone."

"I know that already. But I can start, can't I? We can make an imprint in this mess somehow."

Lai-Kuuvalu said with cold contempt, "For starters? Get your trash out of the ocean."

"Clean up the beaches, got it, we can start with that." He speedily jotted it down on his notepad and then tapped his pen twice to the page. "But who do we get to do it?"

She raised an eyebrow at him. "Who? It should have been done right along, by everyone."

"Got it, fine the shit out of anyone who is caught littering the beaches for additional revenue." He wrote some more. "This is great, keep going."

"... are you attempting to create legislation based off of my listing of grievances?"

Feodor nodded and gave a thumbs up. "That is PRECISELY what I'm doing, keep at it!" He looked at the page in thought. "On that note, we should have community service be to clean up the beach... yeah. That'll do well." He wrote some more.

"It's not merely that the beaches should be clean, the ocean should be revered as should the rest of life and death."

"You know what that sounds like to me?"

"What?"

"The perfect hippy excuse for a Mermaid Day parade!... why does the room suddenly feel cold?" He looked up at Lai-Kuuvalu and saw the glowing symbol on her cheek, her hair starting to bristle. "Whoa, whoa, I know, it's Posidni, not mermaid! Calm down! This is for normal humans, not humans like me!" The room's temperature warmed back up to its previous levels. Feodor sighed. "You don't need to get so emotional over it."

"Where do I even begin? First of all, I am not emotional. We royals are superior to emotions," Lai-Kuuvalu explained. "Second of all, I do not need to explain myself to you. I disapprove."

"Well, first of all, you are emotional. If you weren't, you wouldn't threaten to turn me into a Teddy-cicle whenever I say something you find less-than-savory." As the room started to chill once more, he quickly added, "You see? You're doing it again!"

"I... I am not," she countered, the room staying chilly, getting neither warmer nor colder. A blue sparkle came to her cheeks and she looked away. It was actually rather pretty, like some kind of blue blush with glitter in it.

"Lai-Kuuvalu," he said, voice gentle. "Now you're displaying you're embarrassed."

"I am displaying nothing, it is strictly your imagination, Feodor."

He couldn't help but smile. She was deadly but... there was something about her. "Come on, let's keep talking green, it'll help you feel less blue."

Lai-Kuuvalu didn't like the way she felt around this human, but she wasn't sure exactly what it was she felt. After all, it was as she said: royal Posidni were above emotions.

07 – Sinking Feeling

The rest of the day, the two spent in deep conversation about what Feodor could do to start to make a mark on the mess man had made. It was going to be a long, slow process, but with some luck, the people of Shoreport would swallow the pill he was going to shove down their throats. When the end of the day came, he wheeled Lai-Kuuvalu out of his office. There sat Leila, staring at the two.

"What?" he asked, staring right back at her.

"You ask me "what," but you were holed up in there all day. You didn't even take a break for lunch. You had me take a message for every call and cancel every meeting," responded a mildly irate Leila.

He didn't want to piss her off, but he couldn't exactly tell her the truth, either. Lai-Kuuvalu spoke up, "He was speaking with someone far more important than anyone who reached out to talk to him."

"Including your father, Mayor?"

"Ah shit, why does he never call me on my cell... thank you for letting me know, Leila."

"I'd have let you know sooner if you actually gave me a minute to speak with you."

"Sorry," Feodor said sheepishly.

"Sorry won't work forever, Mayor. Eventually, you're going to have to do something and make some big decisions. You can't just hide behind the mess the previous mayor left you forever."

"I know... I know. I'm sorry. I'll work on it. Okay? I'll work on it." He rubbed his temples in mild frustration. "We really should be heading out; I'm going to take Miss Fisher to the floatation place in Ocean."

"The what?"

"The floatation tanks… they're good for anxiety."

"She doesn't seem anxious."

Lai-Kuuvalu opened her mouth to speak, but he covered it, fast. "She's anxious. Terribly anxious. That's why she glares at everyone, to keep them away from her. It's easier to keep everyone away than to deal with whatever's going on for her on the inside." He could feel his hand getting colder and colder, starting to develop frostbite.

"You two are closer already than you were with Carlotta when you first introduced her. I don't know what Miss Fisher's role is, but you hold her in high regard… well. Have a good day then, Mayor, Miss Fisher."

"*Thank you.*" He grabbed the handles of the wheelchair and wheeled — no, raced — them out of the office to his car. "Damn it, Lai-Kuuvalu, my hand's freezing, what gives!"

"Do not spout nonsense to save your own tail, or else you will suffer the repercussions."

"I get it, but she's too sharp for me, if I didn't say something she'd catch on, and you don't want that." He opened the passenger door and loaded Lai-Kuuvalu in. He stopped for a moment, cheeks going red, as he looked at her face. She either failed to notice or decided not to react, because she didn't make a comment on it. He went to get her seatbelt on her, but she managed to do it herself. "You're a fast learner."

"I am many…" He closed the door. She stared at him through the window. "… things." She watched him fold up the wheelchair. She placed her hand on the bottom of the window as she thought to herself. *Can I do as my ancestors did? Can I keep our influence on man minimal? Can I save them?* And then, a far quieter, smaller thought. *Can I save him?*

The thought caught her so off-guard and angered her so much that when he opened the door to his car, he was slammed with a blast of wintry air. "Whoa! Hey, Lai-Kuuvalu, calm down."

She quickly took her hand off the window, having been so lost in thought she didn't even recognize he had finished his task and set the wheelchair in the trunk. Lai-Kuuvalu turned to face him. "I *am* calm."

"Your version of calm does not turn my car into the arctic." Feodor got into the car and closed the door. He started up the car, opening the windows which cre-e-eaked in agony against the icing they had taken. "Please be careful. I don't want a new car. I like this one."

She huffed and said nothing, crossing her arms. She looked out the window instead as he started to drive.

"In theory," he explained. "This floatation place should have saltwater tanks that you can lie in and do your mer— posidni thing in."

"In theory?"

"I've never actually been to one before, but if it's all good, that's what we'll do."

As they drove, she looked longingly to the ocean whenever they passed it. He had only seen a look like that before from his parents looking at one another. He found himself missing them, but he couldn't exactly introduce Lai-Kuuvalu to them. Feodor looked at her profile. Her eyes were slightly slanted and had long lashes, and she had high cheekbones with full cheeks. She had full lips and a small chin. Her nose was small, too. He felt an uncomfortable feeling in his chest, looking at her; an uncomfortable feeling that made him want to pull to the side of the road and take her into his back seat. He focused on the road once more, warmth filling his body. He didn't like that feeling. Carlotta had been fun, but even in the beginning, he never had urges like that.

The drive was otherwise silent and uneventful. At the parking lot, he helped her into her wheelchair once more and brought her into the store, if it could be called that.

"Hello!" said the woman standing at the front desk. She had perfectly manicured nails and toenails, a fake tan, henna-red hair, and a too-perfect smile. "Do you have an appointment?"

"I'd like to see one of your floatation tanks before making an appointment."

"Of couuurse, you know, we're very concerned about our disabled guests' enjoyment, so let me put your mind at ease. This way," she said, gesturing, as she walked forward. "How long have you been unable to walk for?"

Lai-Kuuvalu stared implacably at this strange woman, who went ahead and continued talking as they made their way down the hall.

"I imagine it must be hard to not walk, have you considered getting prosthetics? I heard that they make everything easier and you can compete in the Special Olympics then."

The sound of skin hitting skin came from behind Lai-Kuuvalu, and she was pretty sure it was the sound of Feodor smacking his own forehead.

"Here we are... feel free to take a look around!"

The room was surprisingly spacious given the small front, but in retrospect, Feodor found it made sense; the customer wouldn't be waiting long at the front desk, and would be spending their time in the room. In one corner of the room was a small standing shower. In the center of the shower, and in the center of the room, was a drain. And then there was the tank; it was a capsule elevated off of the floor.

"Bring me to the tank." Feodor was used to the lack of please-s and thank you-s already, even if he still found it rude, and simply did as directed. "Open the tank and stand me up."

"Ah, you can't go in unless you've bathed first, and if you

have an appointment," said the woman.

"I'm not going inside." Feodor lifted her under her arms, standing her up. She took a small handful of the water into her hand and tasted it.

The woman shrieked, "What is wrong with you?!"

Lai-Kuuvalu calmly looked at Feodor. "The salt in this isn't the sort that I can survive on. No good."

"Got it, let's go." He helped her back into the wheelchair and began to wheel her out.

The woman followed quickly behind them. "Thank you for your visit, please keep us in mind for all of your floatation needs!" As soon as she was sure they were out of earshot, she took out her cellphone and made a call. "Becky? Oh my gawwwd you won't believe what happened just now..."

Outside of the floatation location, he hurriedly apologized. "I am so sorry about that mess, that was..."

"Not your mess. You are the mayor of Shoreport, not this land-place called Ocean. This is mismanagement by some woman, do not let her shortcomings eat you up."

"Huh. That was surprisingly nice of you."

"It was not "nice," it was the truth. Nothing more, nothing less. It would be wise to not attribute human emotions to my words and actions."

"Fine, I take it back, you're a dick. Feel better?"

"What." Lai-Kuuvalu's eyes widened as she gaped at Feodor.

"You can make an expression like that? Let me get out my phone, I want to save this." When he took out his phone, Lai-Kuuvalu easily smacked it out of his hand. It fell to the ground, screen cracking for the umpteen-billionth time. "Hey! Don't smack my phone!"

"Don't threaten to take my image when I am expressing any emotion and I won't have to."

"At least you didn't…" He thought about it for a moment. Maybe it was better to not mention she hadn't frozen his phone. "… never mind."

"The boy learns."

They arrived at his car, and he did his new ritual of getting her in, folding up the wheelchair, putting it into the trunk, and then getting in on the driver's side. He started up the car after his seatbelt on and glanced at her. "I guess we're going grocery shopping for salt."

"If that is what it takes, yes. You will need a lot."

"I'll set up the tub for you." Feodor shook his head. "It's only been a day, but it feels like it's been a year."

"That would explain the white hair," she said flatly.

"That's not funny, don't joke about that, I don't want any white hair, I'm not old."

"How old is old, for a human?" she mused, looking at Feodor now.

He grumped in response, "Older than me is old."

"You're already older than you were when you made that statement, and you're continuing to get older by the second. You may wish to make a revision."

"I have no need to." The drive to Shoreport was equally uneventful, but he found himself in a better mood than just two days ago. There was something about her that was exciting.

Oh, right. She was a mermaid.

Posidni.

Close enough.

The trip to get the salt was almost comically boring, given how exciting the last two days had been. The ride home, equally so. Once they were inside, he asked her, "Do you want some canned tuna for supper?"

"It will suffice," Lai-Kuuvalu responded. Feodor went and

fetched some cans of tuna which he promptly opened and threw into a bowl for her. He grabbed a spoon and slid it over to her on the table. He went about making his own dinner after. As she ate, she said, "You will be setting up the tub for me as soon as dinner is finished."

"Yes, your majesty," he responded drily.

"Oh, you do know how to properly talk to me after all."

"I was being sarcastic; I have no interest in talking to you like that. Not now, not ever."

"You will," she said with a shrug.

"I doubt it. Severely." He made himself some scrambled eggs for dinner with a side of buttered toast. A quick meal. He sat at the table with her and began to eat. "Will you instantly turn into your Posidni form?"

"As instantly as I please it, yes. We royals have magic that allows us to take human form freely, whereas non-royals have to rely on enchanted items to do so. Those items are, of course, illegal."

"What happens to lawbreakers, anyway? Fine? Community service?"

"Imprisonment or death, depends on the severity of the crime," she said, nonchalant.

It was Feodor's turn to gape. "Are you joking? And what about those that voice disagreement with the crown?"

"Disagreement is bound to occur, so long as no revolts are stirred, it doesn't matter. If they are, that's death, too."

"Holy crap. I wouldn't want to live in the ocean, either! No wonder there are Posidni coming to land in secret!"

Lai-Kuuvalu tilted her head. "What do you mean?"

"I mean freedom to be yourself, freedom to express yourself, freedom to do... a whole bunch of things without worrying about being *killed*. Are you really blind to it?"

"What's there to be blind to? The oceans are the best

places to live on the planet, even with their relative destruction by humankind."

"Fascist mermaids. Posidni are fascist mermaids," Feodor said, flabbergasted.

"What does that word mean? Fascist?"

"I'm going to decline to answer that."

"What about the conversation regarding horns, earlier?"

"I'm going to decline answering that as well. Are you done eating?"

"No," she sighed and continued eating her tuna as he made short work of his eggs and toast.

08 – True Blue Colors

"The plumber is going to have a field day with my house after all is said and done," said a disgruntled Feodor as he waited for the tub to fill with cold water. "Are you sure you want the water cold?"

"We royals do best in cold water."

"Should I throw some ice in?" he asked from his kneeling position.

"Do you have any?" Lai-Kuuvalu asked with a hint of surprise from her seat on the toilet, lid down.

He rubbed the side of his head with a hand. "I do, but I'm not going all the way back downstairs to get ice for you. I feel stupid enough having bought out the stock of salt at the store."

"It was for a good cause. You are helping to keep me alive," she explained.

"Hey... what would have happened if you died, anyway?"

"My mother would flood the planet, no second chances given."

Feodor stared at the water as it filled the tub. It was nearing the top. "Yeah, I suppose she would do that, wouldn't she... you are her daughter."

"It would be an act of war, to kill the Heiress. I am her sole daughter. There is nobody next in line after me," Lai-Kuuvalu said. She thought for a moment, and then corrected herself, "Well, nobody except my brother, but males are insufficient leaders and need women to guide them properly."

"Yeah, I guess—hey! No, men, not males, men, are perfectly capable of leading."

"Like you?" she asked with a drop of coyness to her tone.

"Yeah, like… hey, fuck you, okay, I do my best." He turned off the water before the tub could completely overflow. "Damn it, I waited too long… let me drain some."

"Just add the salt in."

"Are you going to mop my floor when you getting in causes the tub to overflow?" Lai-Kuuvalu opened her mouth to speak, but he cut her off. "No, you're not, that's going to be my job, and I'd rather not have to mop up half the contents of the tub off my floor." He started draining the tub.

"Do you enjoy cutting people off before they can speak? Is all you enjoy the sound of your own voice, Feodor?"

"… shut up." He said with a frown, looking at her. She gave him a knowing look. "I don't actually mean to shut up and not speak. I mean… you know what I mean. Stop that. You're making me feel like an ass."

"You are making yourself feel like a donkey, that is on you."

Finally, the tub was at a level he was hopeful wouldn't overflow when she climbed in. He flipped the switch to stop the tub from draining and started to mix in some of the table salt he had purchased. He noticed her moving out of the corner of his eye and turned to look at her. "Oi, don't you want to wait for me to leave the room first?"

"I am beautiful," she countered, head raised slightly as she pulled off her shirt, leaving her in one of Carlotta's too-small bras. "That I am removing my clothing is not only natural, but you should consider yourself blessed to be before a royal in their natural form."

"Natural form nothing, you look like a human, I'm going to react like you're a human, you should wait for me to leave the room!" he said, rapidly climbing to his feet.

"You have already seen this form naked once before, I do

not understand your hesitance. Furthermore, if the issue is Carlotta, she is neither here nor are you two a couple anymore." She took off her bra without any reservations, but Feodor quickly turned his head away.

"Don't you care I might stare at you?"

"Again, I am beautiful; it is expected for me to be appreciated in all my splendor."

He contemplated the basic white tub before him with a burning intensity becoming of a complex mathematical problem. He rolled up a sleeve and started stirring the salt around. "You're going to need me to hoist you into the tub, aren't you." It wasn't a question; he already knew the answer.

"You will carry me, yes."

"Do you still have that necklace on?"

"My holo-clam? Yes. I'll be making a call on it once I am shaped properly."

"You know, it just dawned on me to ask... are reverse mermaids a thing?" he asked, leaning back, feeling certain he had stirred enough. He stood up and went to her, trying to look away.

"What do you mean by a "reverse mermaid?" And how do you intend to lift me without looking?"

"I'll just... feel..." He paused, red reaching from his cheeks all the way to his ears.

"Thought twice about that, it seems. Just look at me. I will not bite you."

He stole a quick glance, though only to lift her; then he all but threw her into the tub in a rush. Feodor panted and she looked up at him, clearly unimpressed, wet hair in her face. "Sorry. Kind of."

"You will teach me to walk, I refuse to be manhandled again."

"Sure..." he started, however, any further thought he had

was swiftly erased. It all happened so fast, it seemed unreal. Her legs came together and white scales encased in gold quickly spread down her body from just below her belly button. At her ankles, her feet changed into a large flipper that was more akin to a fin, bearing those same scales. Her complexion became subtly blue, then more noticeably so, until there was no question that her skin was indeed that color. From each of her outer forearms extended a fin that was longest closest to the wrist; a pair of fins also presented themselves on her lower-half, not far from her pelvis. Her small ears, too, fanned out into fins. The mark of Neptune appeared on her cheek, a cerulean trident that stood out against otherwise unblemished skin. Her eyes were larger, as were her pupils; her irises were aqua-cyan around the edges, but a deep blue, nearly black, by the pupil. The black color dripped from her hair like ink into the water, revealing a rich kelp green in its stead. Between each finger was now webbing, as well. Her hips were wider, her breasts were larger, her waist was smaller, her neck was longer and slenderer, her cheekbones higher, and the slant of her eyes more pronounced... but all of that seemed so utterly mundane and unimportant to everything else.

There she was.

A real mermaid.

No, a real Posidni.

Sitting in his tub.

He didn't react to her submerging herself wholly into the water and taking off her necklace. He didn't react to the water cresting over the tub's lip and spilling forth onto his floor and socks. Feodor slowly moved to sit on the toilet, reaching for it behind him as he kept his eyes on her the whole time. He was sure if he blinked, she would be gone. The pain in his eyes urged him to, so he did.

She was still there. And real.

Lai-Kuuvalu opened her necklace and spoke without

opening her mouth, underwater. He could hear it clearly, but he couldn't understand it at all. She sounded like a chorus unto herself, transcendent harmonies and warm melodies coming together in unison to craft the most wondrous sound that had ever graced his ears. Tears trickled down his cheeks, which he didn't even acknowledge.

If only he knew all she said was "Call Lai-Mefore."

09 – The Call

At her command, a thin, yellow, holographic ring appeared floating over the open clam shell. The ring fluctuated in sine waves as it spoke back to her. "Calling Lai-Mefore."

Eventually the ring changed, taking on the shape of a handsome Posidni man's face in full color. There was no question, looking at that face, that he was a relative of Lai-Kuuvalu, save his eyes which were ice cold in hue and gaze. He even had the same birthmark, or Feodor at least assumed that trident was one. Feodor sat at the edge of his seat, utterly entranced by the unusual communication going on before him. He didn't expect her mouth to be closed the whole conversation, but there she was, making beautiful music from her chest.

"Brother," she said. "I am reporting my well-being and safety."

"Understood, though this trip of yours is truly a folly, sister."

Her face remained the same, but the pitch of her music modulated. "Did I ask you?"

"I suppose not. A whole year up there. You will become jaded yet. I did not think you the starry-eyed optimist… or perhaps you are a boat stalker?"

Her musical voice became harsh as she spoke firmly, "Do not dare spread such nonsense or it will be your end."

"I am afraid I am not quite ready to meet my end, dearest sister."

She exhaled a sigh, singing continuing right through it. "That is a shame, given you are so detestable."

"Detestable! Be still, my heart." Although she could not see it, she was certain that Lai-Mefore put a hand on his chest.

"Will you or will you not relay to Mother-Queen that I am alive and well?"

"I will if you demand it," he responded.

"Then, I demand it."

"It shall be done. Now, about us being something more..."

Before her brother could speak another word, she closed the clamshell pendant, thereby ending the call. She gave the necklace a distasteful look before putting it back on. Her eyes fell on Feodor, sitting on the toilet, tears streaming down his face. "Are... you all right, Feodor?" she asked in English. It felt awkward to ask, but she had never seen someone just sit and sob before.

"You were right," he said softly. "Everything about you is beautiful. Everything about your kind is beautiful."

"Not everything, but close to it." Though speaking English, she was still speaking through her chest, rather than through her mouth. It gave her words a kind of musical accent, and sometimes, a little bit of that choral effect.

Feodor got up and went to the tub. He sat on the lip of the tub, which luckily was just wide enough for it to not be awkward. He gazed down at her and found himself smiling, though he couldn't help it. She wasn't aware of her own natural response, which was a sparkling, dazzling, intense blue coming to her cheeks. It made him smile more. "You look far prettier than Ariel, clam-bra be damned."

"A clam bra? That sounds uncomfortable. Perhaps someone not of the Royal Pod would wear one, but not I."

"Are those a thing? And Royal Pod... is that what the group of royals are called?"

"Yes, clam bras are a thing. I have no idea why they are, or why anyone would willingly wear one, but they are a thing.

Non-Royals wear them, of course, as we royals have no need to adorn ourselves in gaudy items like jewelry or clothing. As for the Royal Pod, yes, that is what the group that comprises the royals are called. But royalty does not work for us as it does for humans."

"I see," he said simply. Lai-Kuuvalu felt a little dejected that he didn't ask for details. But then he seemed to switch topics. "The man on the phone with you before."

"My brother. What of him?"

"What did you two talk about?"

"The usual. I told him I was safe and sound and to report it to my mother, the Queen. He tried to convince me I should take him as a husband. Well, he was going to suggest that, but I did not allow him to get that far. I ended the call."

Feodor blinked a few times in pointed surprise. "Is that normal? Brother and sister..."

"To keep the royal lines pure, yes," she responded. Feodor made a gagging motion. "Not that I have any interest in him. I know his interest in me is purely political, and we direct matrilineal descendants of the Queen do not pick our husbands for political gain. Or in my case, it would be political loss."

"You really are an enigma, you know that?"

"You are not the first, and I doubt you will be the last, to feel that way," said Lai-Kuuvalu. She began to wonder if perhaps her brother was right. Was she just a dreamer, floating in the starry sea of possibilities, reaching only for those bright, shining lights of better tomorrows? Was she truly oblivious to those black holes of deep despair, whirlpools of never-ending doom and destruction?

Was it not true that humans were thinking, feeling beings as well? Did they not cry, did they not bleed? Even if the color of their blood was different than her own, that they bled was enough for her. They spoke, they laughed, they made merry. They argued, they wept, they felt sadness. Were they inferior to Posidni? Absolutely. But there was still something about them...

About the way that he looked at her, right this moment.

She felt something in her chest and quickly covered her heart. The water and room got significantly colder as she glared at him. *No*, she thought. *No, I will not allow that.*

"Brr... everything okay, Lai-Kuuvalu?"

"Your staring is becoming a nuisance. I understand you appreciate my form, but enough is enough."

He sighed and asked, "How long do you intend to stay in there?"

"As long as I please."

"Well, I can't sit here all night long waiting for you to finish up. I have things I'd like to do, and if those things can't include looking at you, then you need to hurry it up in there."

She smacked her flipper in irritation, making water splash up. "Ah! Damn it, Lai-Kuuvalu, now I'm wet!"

"There are worse things than being wet. Perhaps you should embrace being wet instead."

"It's cold, there's no way I'd embrace being wet."

"Maybe," she said coyly. "But maybe you are wrong."

"We'll see."

"You will have to embrace being wet in order to lift me out of the tub."

"Nope, you're going to dry yourself in there before I take you out," he said with a shrug. "Are you ready now?"

She frowned and gave a small nod. "I will never be ready to be a land-dweller, but for this moment, yes, I am ready."

He flipped the switch to drain the tub, fetching a towel right after. By the time he turned to face her once more, she was in her human form.

10 – Shinshin

The days bled together like watercolor on canvas, and before they knew it, Lai-Kuuvalu had already been there for two months. It was a Sunday that he was sitting in his armchair, across from her, as she lay across his couch. She was most comfortably lying with her legs together and had repeatedly turned down wearing either underwear or pants of any kind. After seeing her tail a few times now, Feodor got it; it was uncomfortable to even wrap her head around, even if she'd never say as much.

Lai-Kuuvalu was reading one of his books when she heard a disapproving cluck of the tongue from Feodor. She brought her attention to him, holding a book of his own, and then followed his gaze to the window where she saw what he did. Large, white flakes were drifting down from the sky and clinging to everything they touched. She gasped and shakily got to her wheelchair before Feodor could move or comment, setting her book down on the couch. Lai-Kuuvalu wheeled herself to the window and gazed out at the falling snow.

She had never seen snow like this before. It was true, she had seen snow, and had seen blizzards, but as a royal, she had neither reason nor desire to drift close to shore. Instead, she was treated to the vision of the world outside becoming coated in thick snow. She went to place a hand on the window, but retreated when she realized it was cold. She sped her wheelchair to the front door, opening it, and wheeling herself outside. His interest was piqued; he got up and followed her outside, throwing on his coat.

Feodor opened his mouth, planning to warn her of getting sick due to the cold. Instead, his breath caught, and he gasped at what he saw. She looked in her element, a hand outstretched to the sky to catch the falling snowflakes. Some clung to her hair and lashes, standing out in stark contrast. Her lips took on a richer, bluer shade, and her thinned pupils made her eyes look almost like an icy Mariana Trench. Lai-Kuuvalu would have only looked more stunning in her true form, and he found himself desiring to see her as she truly was, once again. He saw it every day, now, but every day was not enough.

He slowly approached her and reached a hesitant hand out to touch hers. She was surprisingly warm, given how cold it was, and how cold of an act she could put on. He relished in the feeling, but surprisingly found his hand neither grasped nor smacked away. The sound of the world around them faded away, leaving only the snow to discover their secret and keep it silent.

Feodor leaned down and in, placing his lips to Lai-Kuuvalu's.

In truth, the kiss only lasted a second, but it felt like it could have lasted for an eternity. He pulled back from the kiss and looked at her face and into her eyes, searching for something. Her hand went onto her chest... and then her other hand went onto his, grabbing his coat and pulling him closer. Their lips were close, but not touching. He could feel her warm breath against his, and felt every urge to lean in and kiss her once more.

She leaned in further... and placed her forehead against his. No sound escaped her, although that mark had appeared on her cheek, glowing. She held her chest more tightly, and for a brief moment, seemed to be in pain. He leaned back and lifted her out of the wheelchair, into his arms. Feodor pushed the wheelchair back into the house using his legs, and brought her inside as well. With a simple kick of his foot behind him, he closed the door to his house.

A few unsteady steps later, he was sitting on the couch, holding her in his arms. It might have been that he had gotten stronger, though he came to think it was just as likely she had lost weight. He shook that thought from his mind, deciding he would serve her more food going forward. Perhaps, a few months ago, Feodor would follow it up with a thought of not wanting to incur the anger of a Queen who would be happy to see his entire species erased from the surface of the planet, but that was no longer the case for him. He placed his head against hers and rocked her.

Lai-Kuuvalu's head gradually drifted until her ear was square on his chest. Her eyes closed part way. She was certain she heard a beautiful tune mixed in with the lubdubs of his beating heart. Her eyes closed half-way as she rested against him, the pain in her own chest easing as Feodor's grew. He wanted to hear more of her talk-singing, he wanted to hear it with all his heart, directed at him. That desire grew and grew, and so, again, he kissed her. And again, she did not turn him away.

Far from it.

11 – Wait, What?

Everything in his body ached for nothing more than to continue sleeping in the tub on top of Lai-Kuuvalu. Alas, it was Monday, and Feodor was the mayor. The one who decided whether or not kids or their parents had to go to school or work. And he was running way too late to give everyone the day off for the snow that was mostly-melted.

He slowly climbed off of her, out of the tub, and looked down at her sleeping face. She looked ethereal, her hair floating about her in the water. Feodor took this rare moment to admire her resting face and found himself grinning like a fool. That icy core had shattered beneath his touch. But his chest hurt so much... it felt like he was choking, though he was able to breathe just fine.

When they had come together as one, she had sung this sublime song for him. He was too taken by it, by the experience of being face-to-face with her, of seeing a tender expression replace that mask of uncaring indifference. He reached into the water and gently stroked her cheek, which elicited a small clip of song from her. Feodor didn't understand what the song meant, or how it was she was able to sing it even in her sleep, but it made him want to hold her. And so, he did. He lifted her from the water and sat on the floor of the bathroom, cradling her in his arms.

It was only a few minutes of relative calm and peace before she came to. Her eyes opened and she looked up at Feodor, who smiled down at her. Blue came to her cheeks, making them sparkle. "Good morning, Princess."

"Good morning, Teddy," she responded sleepily. For the

briefest of moments, a faint smile had graced her lips… it vanished just as soon as it had appeared. "You have more work today, yes?"

"Every weekday. To your human form so we can get you changed for the day."

"I tire of wearing Carlotta's clothing. I will be supplied with my own."

"You want to go clothes shopping? Sure, we can do that, after work." He placed a kiss on her cheek.

She craned her head back to look at him, bewildered. "Did I give you permission to do that?"

"You did yesterday."

"Yesterday was… yesterday," she said slowly.

Feodor sighed and smiled at her anyway. "Yesterday was amazing. But I understand. Only with your permission, going forward."

"Thank… that is as it should be."

"I heard that. You almost said "thank you!" It *is* in your vocabulary!"

"You are mistaken, Teddy. I would never thank anyone less than the Queen."

His heart skipped a beat. She called him by his nickname, though he had rarely used it in front of her. "I understand, Lai-Kuuvalu."

"When we are alone… just Kuuvalu," she said quietly.

He canted his head slightly. "The "Lai" isn't part of your name?"

"It is a title used by all royals."

"What's it mean?"

"The literal translation of it is "beloved.""

"Beloved Kuuvalu… I approve of the meaning."

She raised an eyebrow in an atypical display of emotion.

"I do not recall asking for your approval of my name or title."

"Never mind that. Let's get going for the day."

He helped her pick out her clothing for the day. The choice seemed to be a pair of faux-fur lined boots with a white faux-fur lined red velvet dress. No matter what she wore, she was gorgeous. As she finished getting changed, he asked, "Today you're calling your mother instead of your brother, right?"

"Correct, today I am reporting directly to my mother. Would you care to be present for the call?"

"I can meet the Queen that easily?"

"You are a politician here on land, you hold some standing, however minor."

"Gee, thanks," he said, shaking his head. "Yeah, I'd like to be part of the call."

"A quiet part of the call."

"Yes, a quiet part of the call, don't worry, I won't talk. I don't want to say something that accidentally causes your mother to murder us all faster." Feodor went over to her and lifted her into his arms once more. He carefully descended the stairs, more carefully than he normally would for fear he might drop her.

"I still think you are all savable."

"What gives you that idea?"

"Well, minus the fines, the people of Shoreport have responded well to your legislation to keep the beaches cleaner, have they not?" Lai-Kuuvalu asked. It was true, the beautification of the beaches was actually a resounding success for something that had just started, and people were eager to get community service cleaning the beach rather than other tasks. "And the preparations for this... Mermaid Parade... have already begun as well."

"Yeah, they have. You're right. Things are looking up." He got her into her wheelchair and then to the car. Once she was all set up and the wheelchair was in the trunk, he climbed into the car.

"Teddy, you have forgotten something important, being a lesser male."

"What?" he asked, staring at her.

"Your clothing."

"Ah dammit. I hope nobody saw me!" He rushed out of the car and ran back into the house. Lai-Kuuvalu smiled to herself for a moment and shook her head. When he came back, he was dressed for work. He climbed into the car and cleared his throat.

"You failed to even notice you were cold; are you feeling well?"

"My brain's a little scrambled from yesterday, but yes, I'm fine otherwise. Great, even." He closed the door, got on his seatbelt, and started driving.

Once they arrived at the office, Leila got his attention. "Mayor, you have a visitor waiting for you in your office." Seeing his eyebrows shoot up in surprise, she continued, "A man by the name of James Hauer."

"James Hauer... Mr. Hauer?" Feodor asked for confirmation. It couldn't be, could it?

Leila nodded. "He said he was your high school English teacher and wanted to see his former student."

"Thank you... wow. Talk about a blast from the past. Let's go, Ariel." Feodor wheeled Lai-Kuuvalu into the office. She knew she'd have to ask him later what exactly high school was. Maybe a group of elevated fish? Elevated fish teacher? That made just about as much sense as half the things she had learned about on land.

Sitting in front of the desk was a heavyset older man. He was bald, with big thick glasses, and he had a beard, mostly gray with a little brown. On his right hand he wore a ring with a red rose on it. "Teddy P.!" The man got up and extended his hand to

Feodor, which he took and shook firmly.

"Mr. Hauer, what an unexpected visit. What brings you here? I hope I didn't make a grammatical mistake in one of my speeches or something."

"Please, call me Jim," he laughed. "You're not a kid anymore."

Kuuvalu sat in her usual regal position, icily regarding this... Jim. He released Feodor's hand and nodded his head to her. "Miss Fisher, it's a pleasure to meet you," he said.

"I do not recall introducing myself. It is a pleasure to meet you as well." She inclined her head slightly in return. Very slightly. Feodor knew she didn't dip her head fully to anyone, except, he surmised, her mother. Feodor closed the door behind them.

"There are... some things we need to talk about." Jim took a seat once more, hands on Feodor's desk. His fingers were curled such that the light reflected off of his rose ring. "If you could ask the secretary to not allow any disturbances, that would be helpful."

Feodor reluctantly obliged; he wheeled Lai-Kuuvalu behind his desk, and then sat in his chair. He dialed Leila and said, "Take a message if anyone needs me until further notice. Thank you, Leila." He hung up right after and gave Jim a small nod.

"Thank you. I'm with a secret society known as the Ordo Rosarius, the Order of the Rose. We've been around for... a long time. Protecting the order of the world and the greater cosmos, both physical and spiritual." He showed them his ring. It was a silver ring with a flat art deco rose embellishment, made of rose gold. "This is our symbol. I've come here, both to talk about protecting humanity from flooding or invasion, as well as to tell you... something that's been kept from you, but will no longer seem so strange now."

Lai-Kuuvalu glared at Jim and opened her mouth slightly. She was ready to sonar blast this man if need be.

"I have some interesting news for you as well, Lai-Kuu-valu," Jim said, dropping his pretenses.

"Speak," she said.

"Teddy's father is a mer."

"Is this some attempt at human humor? If so, it is not very good," Lai-Kuuvalu responded.

Jim said, "I assure you, Lai-Kuuvalu, I am quite serious." He lifted his hand and reached across the desk, pressing his ring to Feodor's cheek. He chanted, "Levate velum. Ostende sit in insigne regis."

Feodor's cheek tingled, and a cerulean trident mark appeared on it.

12 – Part of Your World

Kuuvalu saw the mark and gasped. She grabbed Feodor's head and pulled it towards her, eying the mark on his cheek. "You... you are... you are even a royal!?" she exclaimed in surprise, unable to restrain her emotions.

Feodor got his head from Lai-Kuuvalu's hands and wobbled into his seat. The mark was already starting to fade from view. "I'm... a Posidni? A royal?"

"Yes... you are like me. A true Posidni, not a miposidni. Your name would be Lai-... something." Lai-Kuuvalu looked at Jim. "What was his father's name?"

"Lai-Orani," Jim replied.

"Lai-Orani..." she repeated, and traced in the air. "My mother's cousin's son." Lai-Kuuvalu faced Feodor and smiled brightly. "We're even related!"

"Why... are you smiling? Why is that a good thing? I'm confused and trying not to faint."

"To begin with, that means that turning you into a Posidni is a far easier task; it will only require removing your glamour, which requires significantly less energy. It also means yesterday was far less shameful than I had been concerned about."

"Oh, I'm sorry, what about yesterday was shameful, exactly?" Feodor asked testily, though he looked worse for wear.

"The fact I could have been impregnated by a human," she said simply, hands folded neatly on her lap. "Our child, I suspect, is likely to be royal like we are, instead. This is monumental, joyous news worthy of celebration. So, is this all you came for?"

"No," said Jim. "Not only—"

"... pregnahh..." Feodor fainted, head thudding face-first onto his desk.

Jim and Lai-Kuuvalu were quiet for a time.

Finally, Lai-Kuuvalu spoke up. "I... suppose you will want him conscious for this, will you not." It was less a question and more an acknowledgement of the obvious.

Jim sighed. "That would be nice."

She lifted one hand, and ice grew across it like a thick glove. She placed her hand on the back of Feodor's neck, making him jump. "OW! COLD! OW!" She brought her hand back, ice melting away to water which pooled into a puddle on the ground. "Why... I thought he was Russian... I... I thought he said... he had been adopted by a Russian family..."

"He was arranged to marry Lai-Kuuvalu's mother, the Queen of the Posidni, Lai-Zemforau. He fled up here, and we gave him a new identity. I personally trained him in living like a human, and we became friends. He met your mother, and fell in love with her." Jim smiled softly at Feodor. "He asked me and the other members of the Order to watch over you, which is why I was your teacher."

"My mother has never mentioned this," Lai-Kuuvalu said with a level of uncertainty.

Jim laced his fingers together pensively. "Mention how the man she was supposed to marry her escaped? Why would she?"

"That is a good point. My mother has three husbands, and she has made a point to proclaim not one is the King, not even my own father..."

"How does she decide which one's the king, anyway?" asked Feodor, looking at Lai-Kuuvalu.

Lai-Kuuvalu faced Feodor as she answered, "Usually, the Queen decides by who she is compelled to sing a heartsong for the most."

"Heartsong? Is... that what that singing you do is called? When we..." He trailed off. Lai-Kuuvalu shot him a glare, and the room got colder. "... I got it, I got it, I won't talk about it..." He paused. "What... wait a second. You mentioned removing my glamour... and you've sung your heartsong for me... does that mean I will be the next king, once your reign begins?"

Lai-Kuuvalu nodded her head twice, the faintest of blue blush to her cheeks. She added, quietly, "Beatriz... I hope I get to meet her someday. It would be an honor. Though she raised her son a little too much like a woman, I was able to get him back into tip-top male shape."

Jim laughed drily. "You and the uwan both, all flipped-over with that kind of stuff."

"I suppose you would rather live as the Lunarians do?" she mused.

Jim shook his head. "I wasn't complaining, just noticing it. It's no wonder Neptune's talking to them."

"Hold the phone, what's this about uwan, Lunarians, and Neptune?" asked Feodor.

"Well, I know nothing about the uwan," mumbled a discontent Lai-Kuuvalu. "What else did you come for?"

"I came to tell you that what you two are doing is essential for the continued safety of the human species, as well as other non-human beings, and artifacts. As well as to openly offer my help, and that of the Order." Jim said, twiddling his thumbs.

Kuuvalu placed two fingers to her left temple, leaning her head into her hand. " ... we already knew that for the first part. My mother wants to drown the planet. Neptune wants her to drown the planet but hadn't contacted her before I came to land. And apparently this uwan group wants to buy Earth from Neptune and Neptune is considering it."

Feodor stared at Lai-Kuuvalu, eyes wide as the Moon.

"When were you going to tell me this? When did you find this out?"

"A couple of weeks ago. There was no point in mentioning it to you, there is nothing you could do about it one way or another, aside from continuing as you were with leading the humans in a good way."

"Who exactly wants to buy our planet?" Feodor asked, gaping. "I thought Posidni were... y'know... mermaids. It sounds like you're talking about aliens."

"The Posidni on Earth are descendants of those on Neptune; they're called Neptunians in your language."

"But you do magic," he countered.

"That we royals do, indeed."

"You can't do magic and be descended from aliens."

"Ah, but I am, and that is the end of that discussion."

Feodor gaped at her, and then tried to formulate a sentence. Finally, he managed, "Well, I mean, how about the fact aliens are looking to take over the planet? Who exactly is it?"

"Tsewa? Tsiwa? Some uwan group. Apparently, our distant relatives back on Neptune do not like the damage the humans have done either. "

Jim spoke up now, sitting comfortably in his seat. "The Seventh Empire of Tsewa. Like humans, the uwan aren't one united nation, but the Seventh Empire is one of the more powerful ones."

Kuuvalu's lips turned down into a disapproving frown. "That is idiotic; how do they keep everyone in line?"

Jim offered a tense smile, no longer looking comfortable. He climbed out of his chair. "If you need help, here's my card." He fished around in his pocket and then handed over a small pale pink business card to Feodor. "Just give me a call."

"Thank you, Jim. Take care."

"You too." With that, Jim escorted himself out.

13 – Xenodiplomacy

When he was sure the door was closed and they were alone, Feodor looked at Lai-Kuuvalu. "Explain. Now."

"Explain what? And who do you think you are to command me?"

"Your future king, potentially!"

"Kings are lower on the social hierarchy than Queens or even Princesses, so you may wish to try again, Teddy," Lai-Kuuvalu responded, eyes sparkling with amusement.

Feodor got up and started pacing. "Fine, whatever, *please* tell me what the Hell is going on in a way I can understand."

"That requires some history, I'm afraid, and I know how loathsome humans find history," she said.

"Give me the abridged version, then, something I can swallow."

"I will try, but my success is not guaranteed." She sighed and began, "A long time ago, before the dawn of humanity, my ancestors dwelled on Neptune. There was a major sociological shift at the time to emulate the Saturnines, and the Neptunians were very, very inspired by them. A group of them came to earth and crafted the first proto-cephalopods."

"Back up again," Feodor interrupted. "Saturnines?"

"The people who dwell on the planet Saturn."

"Okay... so your ancestors, from Neptune, were inspired to create the first squids or... something. What does this have to do with what Jim said?"

"You wish to know how the Neptunians are trying to decide the fate of the Earth, do you not? And the relation between the Neptunians and the Posidni?"

Feodor rubbed his forehead. "Which one does your story with Saturn answer?"

"It starts to answer the latter question."

"Okay… go on. Saturn. Neptunians visit earth. They make squids or something. Got it."

Lai-Kuuvalu nodded her head. "The Neptunians were keeping their creations as pets. The Saturnines saw them, liked them, and decided they would ascend them from being pets into being thinking, feeling, speaking creatures."

"Whoa. Okay. So, the Saturnines are more technologically advanced?"

"Yes," Lai-Kuuvalu said. "When they were ascended, they took on the name of Kfalli for themselves."

"Let me see if I follow: the people from Saturn saw that the Neptunians had made squids in their likeness or something, and were like, "Ooh, they're like us, so let's make them people" and turned the squids into Kfalli."

"Something like that. Then, some group of Neptunians got it into their head to…" She shuddered. "… breed… with the Kfalli."

"Well, I mean, tentacles, so…" started Feodor. He stopped when he saw the intense, disapproving stare Lai-Kuuvalu was subjecting him to. "… go on."

"This was an affront to the Neptunians, but also to nature itself. We had *created* the Kfalli, those Neptunians had no business *breeding* with them," Lai-Kuuvalu explained. "Thus, those Neptunians, the Kfalli involved, and their offspring were banished to Earth… along with…" She inhaled as she said, "… my direct ancestor, the sister to one of Queen of Neptune's ancestors."

"That means there's a little Kfalli in you?"

"My blood is pure," She cut him off abruptly with a frown. "Hundreds of thousands of years of mating and birth led to my existence, hundreds and thousands of years with no Kfalli intermingling, just the occasional miposidni."

"Now, what's the difference between a Posidni and a miposidni?"

Lai-Kuuvalu tapped her cheek, where her mark of Neptune would be. "The symbol of our ancestors."

"... that's it?"

"That is it."

"Now I have even more questions... why does it seem the questions never end?" Feodor asked, rubbing his head in apparent frustration.

"You are learning about a new culture. It is normal to have questions. It is better to ask them now, rather than make a fool of yourself when you go to the oceans, where you belong."

"Kuuvalu, there is nothing, there is nobody, that could convince me to go to the oceans."

"We will see yet, Teddy, we will see yet."

He shook his head. "What does the mi- in miposidni do?"

"It denotes being lesser, being below."

It was Feodor's turn to stare at Lai-Kuuvalu. "... you call the Posidni born without the mark of Neptune sub-posidni. That's... that's fucked up."

"It is the way things are. It is the way things will continue to be, to maintain the careful balance within our seas that we have managed. I will have you know, we are more tolerant than Neptune is. Then again, Neptune is the first line of defense against foreign invaders."

"You mean... other aliens." He paled. "Neptune has been keeping us humans safe all this time by keeping out aliens?"

"Aside from their initial failure against the predecessors to the Solarians, yes," said Lai-Kuuvalu.

Feodor paced from one end of the room to the other, then turned after reaching the wall. "There are sun-aliens too?"

"Solarians. Yes. Very violent. Conniving. I wouldn't suggest dealing with them if possible. They're too obsessed with Lun right now to bother with Earth and its inhabitants."

"Lun. Lunarians. People on the Moon, too. How the Hell are they hiding? I mean, we've sent people to the Moon, and there's no water or any signs of life."

"They live beyond the veil, though there is water on the Moon. Beyond the veil, plenty of life and water, actually," said Lai-Kuuvalu matter-of-factly.

He pinched his nose. "It sounds like half of this stuff is made up. There's no way this solar system is this crowded and humanity has been left in the dark all this time."

"Humans are rather dense on the whole, you forgot about people living in your oceans," she responded knowingly, watching Feodor's face flush with anger.

"You don't get to criticize us, you come from a group of race purists!"

"Yes, so race purist that I slept with you," she countered.

He held up his pointer finger as he stomped his foot. "You're the exception, not the rule, and even then, you were *happy* that I was a Posidni like you are, rather than a non-royal Posidni."

"A miposidni," she said patiently.

"No," he said, raising his voice. "No, I am not calling them that. And you shouldn't call them that either."

"What should I call them then? Would you rather I pluralize the royal title and negate it?"

"That's still fucked up, that's saying they're not beloved!" he stomped his foot again in anger. "You can't treat a whole group of people like that!"

"Humans have done it before as well."

"They still do, it doesn't make it right! Haven't you learned "two wrongs don't make a right?!"" he asked, messing his own hair in righteous anxiety.

She stared at him for a long moment. "As I was saying: ever since those Neptunians, Kfalli, and their children, the Cephaloi, were banished to Earth, Neptune has felt a level of responsibility for those of us on this planet. They have sought to keep us safe and alive, while influencing the local life and its evolution as little as possible. Our creation of the proto-cephalopods led to the eventual birth of the first cephalopods. We swore to keep off of land and away from whatever came to be outside of the seas. Everything was going according to plan until the humans came about. Posidni were fascinated by this juvenile species, and humans were taken by our beauty. Still, we mostly kept to ourselves. Enough to have become myth to man.

"This was fine, until mankind began severely polluting the very waters we breathe. I suspect it was at this point there was discussion of whether or not to leave the humans be. Again, and again, it seems the decision was ultimately to leave them alone and allow them to come to the realization on their own that they should not be harming the waters we breathe or the air they breathe."

"Well, that was a mistake," mumbled Feodor. "Humans aren't exactly known for being introspective or giving two shits about anybody besides themselves. Quite frankly, it's kind of amazing that after all this time, Neptune still cares about you Posidni here on Earth."

"My hunch is that Neptune has finally caught wind of the damage being done to the planet and is looking to do something about it to save the Posidni so we do not die at humanity's hands."

"Let me recap... some Neptunians thought it would be a good idea to create a whole new species based off of a group of aliens called Saturnines, the Saturnines made this species able to operate as their own people called Kfalli, some other Neptu-nians decided to fuck them, and they all got sent to Earth by one of the fuckers' big sister, who was the Queen of Neptune. Because of this, Neptune views Posidni – which are not Neptu-nians, but descended from them – as their little sister and is looking to protect them from the big bully that is humanity. Which somehow leads us to Neptune looking to sell the planet to *yet another* group of aliens, called uwan."

"That sounds about right," Lai-Kuuvalu said, tapping her lips.

Feodor concluded, "In short, we're fucked."

14 – Mind Your Mind

The rest of the day had been a blur for Feodor. He was glad Lai-Kuuvalu was there to help him with managing his meetings, and that Leila was there to cut down the number of meetings he had in the first place.

All he could think about was the fate of humanity.

The Queen of the Posidni wanted to flood the planet and kill most of humanity off in one fell swoop. The Queen of Neptune wanted to sell the planet to the uwan – specifically, The Seventh Empire of Tsewa. And Lai-Kuuvalu was... possibly a racist fascist mermaid?

"... r... dor... Feodor. Feodor."

"Huh?" He came back to reality and looked down at Lai-Kuuvalu.

"The work day has come to an end. It is time to bring me shopping for clothing, so I no longer have to use Carlotta's."

"Oh... right." He took her chair and wheeled her out of his office and into his secretary's. Leila looked up at him.

"Heading home, Mayor?"

"What?"

"Shopping," Lai-Kuuvalu corrected. "He is going to get me some clothing of my own."

Leila looked at Feodor. She couldn't help but notice the way he stared forward at nothing in particular, like he had seen something terrible beyond imagination. Shellshocked. He looked shellshocked. She didn't particularly like Feodor in the beginning, and it was only since the arrival of the mysterious Ariel Fisher that he started behaving in a way she could consider worthy of being a mayor. What could his former teacher have told him that left him looking like he had been to Hell and back? "Don't run the poor man broke, we pay him well, but the taxpayers may faint if they see their hard-earned cash going towards your wardrobe."

"I will buy nothing excessive, only that which accentuates what I already have."

"What happened to your clothing, exactly? Are they hand-me-downs?"

That brought Feodor back for the moment. "Yes! Yes. Kind of. They're hand-me-ups from Carlotta, who she doesn't want to rely on any further."

"To be honest, I'm glad neither of you are looking to rely on Carlotta anymore. That woman had an attitude issue. I heard that she—"

"Leila," said Lai-Kuuvalu. "Gossip is unbecoming of a woman. It is better to leave that nonsense to the males." Feodor cleared his throat. She rolled her eyes and corrected herself. "To the *men*."

"Men, gossipy? Where are you from?"

"Oh-kay, we have to go now, have a great evening!" He quickly wheeled Lai-Kuuvalu out of the office towards his car. "Can't you talk without being suspicious?"

Lai-Kuuvalu turned her head a little to the left, then a little to the right, causing her hair to toss about. "I am not suspicious. I am a perfect specimen of the Posidni."

"Would a perfect specimen of the Posidni have had sex with a human?"

"Ah, but you are not a human, you are not even a mi-posidni, you are a Posidni like I am," she said as he helped her into the car.

"Miss Perfect Posidni, you're going to have to learn to get yourself into the car on your own one of these days."

"Just as soon as you teach me to walk."

He got into the car on his side once the wheelchair was loaded up. He buckled up and stared out his windshield. If she could walk, it would be easier. She would have her freedom to move as she so pleased. But there would also be the issue that those same legs could be used to leave his home and return to the ocean without warning. That she could tell her mother nothing was worth saving after his backtalk and sass, and that he would just wake up one morning up to the neck in water without her anywhere in sight. If she could walk, she could doom humanity.

If she could walk, she could walk right out of his life.

"No..." he said quietly as he began to drive. "No, I don't believe I will."

"Excuse me?" Lai-Kuuvalu said, staring at him. "I believe you just said you will not teach me to walk."

"You heard me right, I'm not going to teach you to walk. I'll deal with lifting you. Besides, shouldn't royalty keep their feet off the ground?"

"I don't know your strange human customs for royalty," Lai-Kuuvalu countered with a frown. "But I fail to see why I should be subjected to them."

"You might be right, but that's how I'm going to treat you anyway," he half-lied. Why am I lying to her? Why not just tell her that I'm terrified of her?

Oh yeah, that will go over well.

She was beautiful, but also, slowly, becoming repulsive to him. If they could spend forever wrapped in each other, surrounded by her heartsong, it might have all been okay... before today. But the words of his former teacher filled his mind.

Humanity was relying on them.

Humanity was relying on *him*.

He didn't want to dare include her as one of humanity's

potential saviors. He needed to open her eyes to the injustice she was perpetuating, the injustice she thought was necessary to keep balance within the oceans. She was going to be the next Queen.

It would be easier to turn a blind eye to their plight. But the more he thought of doing it, the more his stomach twisted in knots. They pulled into the parking lot of a dress store. He unbuckled his seatbelt and bolted to the nearest garbage can, emptying the contents of his stomach into it.

Lai-Kuuvalu watched Feodor from her seat in his car. She slowly unbuckled her seatbelt and observed him vomiting. He was supposed to help her save humanity, but she found herself doubting his resolve. He wanted to start a fight with her. She could feel it. He had become too comfortable with her, too used to her presence, to think he could start an argument with her *and win*. What she couldn't grasp was why he wanted to start a fight with her.

Even her brother knew that starting fights with her was a folly, so why did Feodor insist that the beliefs and functions of Posidni were incorrect? The miposidni were lesser, that's why they weren't called Posidni… even then, they *were* called Posidni when grouped with royals, thereby momentarily elevating their status! That was why it was custom for miposidni to give thanks whenever they were referred to as Posidni.

Lai-Mefore was not Feodor. Feodor was not Lai-Mefore. She was grateful for each of these statements being true. Even though that was the case, she found any hints of interest within her heart fading away to give way to Feodor's image. His ungraceful, inelegant image of him throwing up into a large black metal container.

She ended up singing part of their heartsong, unable to help herself. She placed a hand on her heart, as if trying to block the sound from coming out. "Not now," she whispered to herself in her language. "Do not feel that way right now, while he looks like that."

Feodor lifted his head out of the bin, sweating and pallid. "Okay... I think I'm okay..." he gasped out. "I think I'm going to be okay."

15 – Changes

After buying five dresses, he brought the both of them home. From the parking spot, he asked, "Kuuvalu, do you believe you'll ever change?"

"There is nothing for me to change about myself. What about you, Teddy? Do you think you will ever change?"

"I'm worried I might," he admitted, looking at his steering wheel. He put his car into park, turned it off, and took off his seatbelt. Feodor corrected himself, "I'm worried I already have; I don't want to change even more."

"Is changing so terrible, when you are imperfect?"

"Gee, thanks."

Lai-Kuuvalu looked at Feodor. "All except for the royal Posidni are imperfect. It was not an insult; it was sincere."

"Sincerely..." He looked at the roof of his car interior in thought. "Changing sucks, whether or not a person is imperfect."

"Changing only, as you put it, sucks, when you do not anticipate it. All of my changing I did in my youth as my mother molded me into the perfect Heiress. The person you may become, the person you wish to be, the person you are... there are many selves, and rarely do they coalesce into a single form that is who we are."

Feodor furrowed his brow in thought. After a few moments, he commented, "This is too philosophical for me, especially given the weight of today." He opened his door and climbed out.

Lai-Kuuvalu sighed quietly through her nose. *I hope he meditates on my words*, she thought.

Dinner was the Atlantic halibut he had taken out of the freezer last night. She kept emphasizing that the fish was subpar and that should Feodor ever take on his true form, he would experience fish with real flavor. Truth be told, he was simultaneously curious about and horrified by the life to be had beneath the waves.

He thought of all the people of Shoreport he'd be leaving behind, the people relying on him. He knew that they wouldn't re-elect him, so their relying on him would be coming to a fairly expected end, and then they wouldn't give him the time of day. He thought of Carlotta... and then he thought better. He thought of his parents. His father, Lai-Orani. The one who got away.

Feodor began to sweat bullets as he did the dishes. He dropped the plate he was holding, and it shattered in the sink. "Shit," he said under his breath. How would this fascist racist Queen respond to his father being on land, being the one who got away? How would she respond to him, Feodor, even *existing*? He slowly picked up the pieces of plate and threw them into the garbage.

"Teddy? Are you almost ready for the call? I should be in my true form for it. It would be advisable for you to do the same."

"My tub is not big enough for the both of us," he said with a frown.

"You could drive us to the ocean instead," Lai-Kuuvalu suggested.

Feodor snorted. "Oh yes, let's have that make the news instead." He held a hand in the air and brought it across the space before him as he spoke. "Shoreport Mayor Caught Skinny-dipping." He shook his head in the negative as he lowered his arm back down. "That's not happening."

"We can breathe without saltwater... it is just difficult and uncomfortable. You should have an easier time, having some human blood in you. Perhaps we should try your bed instead? Or my bed. I do not have a preference."

"We'll use the guest bed, I guess. I'm not sure I still want to meet your mother."

Lai-Kuuvalu rested her hands on her lap. "It matters not; you are meeting her. If not for me, if not for your political rank, then for the sake of humanity. You are the de facto representative for humanity, you best live up to it."

After finishing the dishes, Feodor took the handles of Lai-Kuuvalu's wheelchair and brought her to the bottom of the stairs. He carefully lifted her into his arms. "I just realized: I won't be able to understand a word you are saying to her."

"I will be translating except when instructed not to translate by the Queen."

"Do you address her as the Queen?" he asked as he climbed the stairs with her in his arms.

"I address her as Mother-Queen," she said. "And when I have a child of my own, they will call me by my title as well, Mother-Heiress, until my mother abdicates the throne. Then I will be Mother-Queen, as she was."

"And others address her as?"

"Queen, Her Majesty, Ruler of the Seven Seas." She gave a slight shrug. "Or those are the approximate translations, at least."

When he arrived at the top of the stairs, he asked Lai-Kuuvalu, "And what will happen to me if I mess up somehow?"

"If my translation is in error, I will be reprimanded, you may be imprisoned. With luck and effort, I will keep us both free from punishment. I ask that you not be so brutish with your line of questioning towards my mother as you are with me. For both of our sakes," she responded.

"If I'm going to be stiff and dying on the inside, I'm doing it in comfort. We're using my bed after all," he said as he led them off to his bedroom. He pushed the door open with his foot and brought her to the bed where he set her down. She immediately began to get unchanged. "Could you at least wait a minute so I can breathe?"

"Are you not breathing currently, Teddy? You should take your clothing off so I can force off your glamour and allow you to take your true form as well."

He sat down on the edge of the bed and stripped down to his underwear. "Can't I do this underneath the blankets?"

"Feodor," Lai-Kuuvalu said a little firmly. "You are not hiding your true form from yourself or from me. Take off your underwear and lay down on the bed, or else when I remove your glamour you're going to slide onto the ground."

"Fine... fine." He removed his underwear as well and stepped his legs up onto the bed. Feodor was perfectly adequate in his shape and form as a human male. He had some light pudge to him, gentle-sloping shoulders, narrow hips, and toned thighs. Despite this, he still looked uncomfortable.

Lai-Kuuvalu took on her true form and looked at Feodor intently, the mark of Neptune on her cheek glowing brightly. As she did, he felt his body begin to change; it was hard to believe what was happening actually was, especially given how fast the transformation occurred. His legs came together and pitch-black scales with sprinklings of silver and gold spread down his body, from the lower half of his torso below his belly button, down. His feet came together at the ankles, changing into a large fin-like flipper with those same scales. Feodor's complexion transitioned into a mother-of-pearl void of white, replaced instead by a blue that bordered on black. From each of his outer forearms extended a fin that was longest closest to the wrist; a pair of fins also presented themselves on his lower-half, not far from his pelvis. His sizable ears fanned out into fins as well. The mark of Neptune appeared on his cheek, a cerulean trident that stood out against the dark hues of his skin. His eyes were only slightly larger, as were his pupils; the result was a pair of jet-black eyes with no distinction between pupil and iris. Unlike Lai-Kuuvalu, there was no webbing between each of his fingers.

As much as he hated to admit it, for the first time in his life, he felt… right. Like he finally was in the body he was supposed to be in. He had always felt off, but he didn't spend any extended amount of time thinking about it. Everyone feels this way, he thought to himself in the past. Or perhaps he was the odd one out and to be normal he had to pretend like there was nothing wrong. But now, finally, he felt right in his own skin. He was free from the body he used to have and, while having a new set of limitations, finally was able to be himself.

"Kuuvalu, I look so… different." He touched his fins, and then his tail, and finally his flipper.

"You are beautiful," Lai-Kuuvalu said softly.

He froze. "Hey, wait a second. Where is my…"

"Beneath your scales," Lai-Kuuvalu sighed, shaking her head. Males.

16 – The Call, Again

"Are you ready for this call?"

"As ready as I'm going to be," he said, breathing with a little difficulty. He hadn't expected to have any issue breathing, despite being warned of its likelihood. It was hard to place, but the air felt almost grainy. It made his lungs tickle in a way he did not enjoy, like he had a cough coming on that wasn't fully there.

Lai-Kuuvalu must have noticed, because she said, "It would not be so laborious to breathe if humanity took better care of their air. Alas, they want to suffocate themselves nearly as much as they wish to suffocate us."

"Don't… remind me. I get it. I should have voted Green… augh, this is the single worst thing about this form."

"You should try breathing the water by the shore. It is nearly as bad. With that in mind, I am going to make my call now. Would you care to move closer?"

He placed his hands on the bed and slowly nudged himself closer to her, until they were touching, side-to-side. A faint smattering of blue came to her cheeks and she looked up at him. A clip of her heartsong came from her chest, and without any effort from himself, he responded with his own clip of heartsong. She blushed more, and the two of them sang with one another, coming to hold each other's hand. At different parts, his heartsong would stop, and hers would fill it in; at others, the other way around; others still, they would sing in harmony. They lay next to each other, singing to one another, holding hands.

Feodor's heart raced and leapt as he sang. That choking

feeling from before was gone. He felt whole. He let himself get swept away by their singing for an uncountable amount of time. All he could do was think of her and gaze into her eyes as they sung. He was starting to feel tired, if very content. She brought her other hand up and cupped his cheek. "Teddy," she said softly. "I have to call my mother. We cannot sing the whole night away."

"Alright," he said, his voice as soft. "We can call your mother now."

She released his cheek and hand and took off her necklace. She opened it up and spoke that beautiful language he couldn't understand. "Call Lai-Zemforau." Once more, a thin, yellow, holographic ring appeared floating over the open clam shell. The ring fluctuated in sine waves as it spoke back to her, "Calling Lai-Zemforau." Feodor was used to seeing this by now, but he had never been allowed into one of the calls.

Lai-Zemforau's face came into view, hovering in place of where the ring had been. "Lai-Kuuvalu. It has been too long."

"Mother-Queen, hail and tidings to you."

Lai-Zemforau turned her head a little and squinted at Feodor. It was remarkable how similar she looked to Lai-Kuuvalu. Despite the age difference he knew had to exist, if he hadn't known better, he would have mistaken them for sisters. "Lai-Orani?" asked Lai-Zemforau.

"Close, Mother-Queen. This is his son, Feodor Neftali Petrov. He is half human," she explained.

"Why is she staring at me like that?" asked Feodor.

Lai-Kuuvalu didn't break eye contact with her mother as she said in English, "You look remarkably like your father, considering you are only half Posidni."

"Have you located Lai-Orani?"

"No, Mother-Queen. Just his son. He is the human in my reports to Lai-Mefore that has been housing me."

"Ah, the lowly Mayor."

"Yes, Mother-Queen."

Lai-Zemforau betrayed no emotion as she asked, "Has your brother seen him as a Posidni?"

"Not yet, Mother-Queen."

"Then what was that boy jealous for? We will have a talk with Lai-Mefore and inform him his worries are well-placed *now*, but were not before."

Lai-Kuuvalu decided to leave out that she had gotten to know Feodor intimately when they were certain he was just a normal human. "Thank you, Mother-Queen. That is exceptionally gracious of you."

"What is his Posidni name?"

Lai-Kuuvalu asked Feodor in English, "My mother wants to know your Posidni name. Did your father give you one?"

"How the Hell should I know?"

Lai-Kuuvalu exhaled a sigh through her nose as she relayed to her mother in that sing-song language, "He knows not his name, nor if his father gave him one."

"A shame. If your current mission were not so urgent, we would have you seek out our Lai-Orani. We suspect he will come crawling out of the caverns on his own soon enough."

"Yes, Mother-Queen."

Lai-Zemforau asked in a calm voice, "Do you think the humans are savable still?"

"Yes, Mother-Queen," Lai-Kuuvalu said, giving the slightest of nods.

"It is unbecoming of you to show such emotions. Being around this Feodor has had a negative effect on you."

"My sincerest apologies, Mother-Queen." Lai-Kuuvalu's face went emotionally flat. Her musical voice became precise, rather than as flowing and fluctuating as before. "Yes, I do believe the humans are still savable. They have shown an interest in cleaning up their beach."

"Beaches?" Lai-Zemforau asked, looking to correct her daughter.

"Beach. Feodor is a mayor, which is like the mayors back home in that he only has domain over one area, not multiple, and his area is Shoreport. Additionally, he lacks control over the humans he does have influence over."

"Influence matters not, power matters. They should listen to his every instruction, as a Posidni."

"The humans have forgotten about the Posidni, and we have become things of myth called mermaids."

"Mermaids… that name again. What a shallow name to have given our people."

"I agree, but it is the name they have for us, and we have not shown our faces to them for quite some time."

"You must speak to the women higher up on the political hierarchy. Feodor is both male and low in the hierarchy, he is but a sardine in the sea of power."

Lai-Kuuvalu restrained her urge to sigh. "Unfortunately, the males on land are the ones in power."

"*Still*? The human women have not sorted that out yet?"

"No, Mother-Queen."

"What a shame. Humans are so weak."

"They are, Mother-Queen."

"Yet, they manage to cause so much damage. You will continue to observe the humans. See if they will follow through with healing their shores. Seek to speak to someone higher up."

"As you command it, Mother-Queen."

"Do something about this male as well. Will he be staying with you?"

Lai-Kuuvalu turned her head towards Feodor, breaking eye contact with her mother. She opened her mouth to ask him… but… decided not to. She looked back to the holographic image of her mother. "No, Mother-Queen. He will be remaining on land."

"He will return to the ocean, as will Lai-Orani, mark our words."

"Yes, Mother-Queen."

"You will take this Feodor as a husband," Lai-Zemforau said with a sense of finality.

"... yes, Mother-Queen."

Feodor perked up and asked, "Why did she look right at me for a second there?"

"Her Majesty decided you're going to be one of my husbands."

"Whoa, whoa, what about what I want?"

"What either of us wants does not matter," Lai-Kuuvalu said, doing her best to mask her own emotions.

"Tell her I said I refuse to marry you."

"I will discuss it with you after." She gave her attention to Lai-Zemforau again. "Thank you, Mother-Queen, for your guidance."

"We look forward to future reports. We will deal with your brother now. Excuse us." The call ended, and Lai-Kuuvalu closed the holo-clam with a *click*!

17 – Not Part of Your World

"What exactly is this about us getting married? I missed the part where I have a choice," Feodor said with a disapproving frown.

Lai-Kuuvalu sighed in a rare display of her own frustration. "Mother-Queen gave neither of us a choice, Feodor. Hold this conversation long enough for me to transform you."

"Wait, I..." And before he could argue, he was human-shaped again. And naked. Very naked. He felt an anger rising up in him. "I said to wait! I didn't want to be human again!"

"You *are* human, you *will always* be human. You just happen to also be Posidni. Why are you upset? I know being Posidni is far superior, but..."

"I barely had any time in that form!"

"Yes, well, I need to be put in the tub or else I am going to get ill and possibly die. We would like to avoid that, would we not?"

"I could have gone into the tub with you!"

"You said it yourself: the tub is too small," Lai-Kuuvalu responded with a sigh.

Feodor got off the bed and lifted her, carrying her off to the bathroom. He set her in the empty tub. It really was too small for both of them. "It's not fair. You have spent your entire life being this, and I only got to spend a few moments."

"I am sorry, I did not want you to die, and upkeeping your own glamour requires energy, which is why you probably have never been into sports or running marathons, if I had to guess." Lai-Kuuvalu was right. He hadn't been into sports, not even as a child. He was tired rather often and relied heavily on shots of caffeine to get through his day at a young age, and even those failed him fairly often.

It didn't matter at the moment. What mattered was he wanted to be himself again. He was human, too, but there was this other part of himself he had only been given a chance to glimpse at. He wanted to explore it to its fullest, to know this other body that was also his, and to understand this secret his father had hidden from him his entire life.

Lai-Kuuvalu turned on the cold water and motioned to one of the containers of salt. He handed it over begrudgingly. "Your mother—"

"Not until I'm underwater, talking hurts enough in the air," she said, speaking through her chest as per usual in this form.

Feodor sighed and watched her stir the salt in on her own. He failed to place the disappointment he felt growing within himself. Perhaps it was a disappointment with himself, that he was so taken by this Posidni woman. If she were human, and if things were as they were before, and if he were talking to some-one else who had feelings for her, he would have told them to keep far away. Falling head over heels for someone like Lai-Kuu-valu would be asking for trouble. Head over fin? *Damn, is that even a saying for Posidni?* he wondered.

Lai-Kuuvalu stared at the salt as it faded into the cold water, slowly dissolving in a cloud. Things were beginning to make less sense for her. She was on land to prove humanity's worthiness, so what was she doing sharing her heartsong with... anybody? No less, Feodor? She added more salt into the water and stirred it in as well. Once satisfied with its salinity, she slid into the water. "Now we may speak, Teddy."

"Don't... call me Teddy right now."

"Feodor, then."

"Yeah," he sighed. "Look, no offense, but I have no intent to marry someone I've only known for two months."

"I have no intent to take you as a husband at this point in time, either," she said coolly.

He raised an eyebrow. "Then, what your mother said…"

"Oh, I cannot disobey her. You, on the other hand, are born of disobedience; you are free to disobey her orders for as long as you can hold out," Lai-Kuuvalu responded.

"The talk earlier with Jim… could you really be pregnant?"

"It is possible."

"I don't want to marry you, but I want to be part of my child's life, if you are pregnant."

"No," she said.

"Thanks for being so—wait, you said no. What do you mean no?" Feodor's gaze could bore a hole into Lai-Kuuvalu. She was unaffected.

Bringing a hand to her womb, she said, "I mean no. If you are not my husband, you are not going to participate in my child's life."

Flabbergasted, he asked, "Then why the fuck did you have sex with me, if you knew we could get pregnant?"

"You knew as well; it was equally your decision. You were not in open opposition to my people or their way of life before. Not nearly as much as you have been in the last twenty-four hours."

"I didn't know just how fucked up they were before! I would never want to be part of your world, knowing what I know now!" The temperature of the room dropped and the water got slushy. He realized his mistake, and began, "Kuuvalu, I…"

"Then live forevermore as a human, Feodor Neftali Petrov. May you never again know my embrace or the embrace of any Posidni or ocean-dweller." Her voice was so beautiful, but her tone so harsh, it was like a siren was cursing him. "May you live a long human life with human experiences."

"I'm sorry. Stop. Please," he begged softly, getting to his knees next to the tub. "You're the only one who I know who can remove my... you called it glamour, right? You're the only one I know, besides maybe Jim, and it would be awkward to ask him to do it. You're the only one aside from maybe my parents who have seen the Posidni-me."

"Ask your father, then. If Lai-Orani is more than capable of giving you a glamour that you have to supplement with your own energy, he should be able to remove it as well, just as I have."

"His name is Renat Petrov... that's the name he wants to be known as."

"He is as much Renat as I am Ariel. It is a made-up name to exist a world we do not belong to, do not belong in." Lai-Kuu-valu said coldly. "And it would be best that you not forget that. I am not the Ariel Fisher you have created; I am Lai-Kuuvalu, Heiress, daughter of Her Majesty, Ruler of the Seven Seas, Queen Lai-Zemforau."

He shivered and hugged himself. This glamour thing must have been strong, because he had a feeling that if he was in his Posidni form, the cold would not affect him nearly as much. "I'm sorry, Kuuvalu."

"Do not call me Kuuvalu. Use my title appropriately."

She felt millions of miles away despite being right in front of him. He was angry. He was sad. His vision was fuzzy thanks to the tears forming in his eyes. He leaned over the side of the tub, slid his hand under her neck, and gently pulled her head up while dipping his head forward to kiss her. The room got colder, and even he swore he was starting to freeze, but he could hear her heartsong in her chest like a whisper. He, himself, felt like he was choking at the chest level again. Now he knew why.

Why do I detest everything she stands for, and still want

to be with her? I'm not comfortable with this.

He slowly broke the kiss and looked down at her face. He was startled to discover tears in her own eyes. One tear went down her cheek, and as it did, it formed into a pearl which plopped into the tub water.

"Why is it like this?" they both asked softly in unison, pulling together so their foreheads nearly touched, separated only by the water.

18 – Christmas Eve

The days that followed were a painful mess marked by silence. Feodor loaded her into the car to get to work, but she didn't speak to him more than she deemed necessary. She gave him clipped answers of yes's and no's, never engaging him in longer conversation even when he offered the opportunity.

When Feodor was returning from a bathroom break at work, Leila stopped him. "Mayor, might I have a word?"

"What's up, Leila?" He felt drained. He hadn't had a chance to go back to his true form. He also had been ignoring his parents' calls. He knew they were getting worried, but the further he kept them from the situation, the better.

Leila leaned over her desk, looking up at him. "It seems to me like you and Miss Fisher are having some issues."

Feodor sagged. "Is it that obvious?"

"From miles away. You know, they say it's going to snow this Christmas, and it's only a few days away. Why not take her out on a date?"

"A date? With K... Ariel?"

"Yes, with Miss Fisher, who else? Take her out for the day and show her a good time. Think about what makes her happy."

Did anything make her happy?

The ocean. The ocean made her happy. It was her home. He had been keeping her from it since he got her from the shore. The realization made his stomach sink. How happy would he be if he was told he never could return home again?

That's exactly what her mother wanted for him. To ban him from returning home ever again and chaining him to Lai-

Kuuvalu.

A small part of his mind whispered, *would that be the worst outcome?* The thought made him shift around slightly, as if trying to shake off something clawing its way up to his chest. It was a warm prickly feeling, and it made him vaguely uncomfortable in ways he couldn't place.

"I'll... try to float that idea past her, but she's a very headstrong woman with her own ideas."

"I know honey, that's why I like her so much. Finally, someone around here who takes the reins."

Or the reign, he thought, a little disappointed in himself. He exhaled a sigh through his nose. "Thanks, Leila."

"Any time."

He went back into his office, closing the door behind him. He leaned back against the door and looked at Lai-Kuuvalu, whose attention immediately settled on him. Before, her cold gaze would have spread chills across his body; now, he could see the hidden meanings in her unspoken words. Come here. Talk to me. And so, he did.

"Lai-Kuuvalu," he said, voice cracking for a moment. "What am I, twelve?" he coughed and tried again. "Lai-Kuuvalu." She raised one manicured eyebrow at him. "I would like us to spend Christmas day together."

"... when?"

"Christmas. You know. The day of Christ's birth? Santa day? Ho ho ho?"

"I know of this Christ, but not what he misses, nor of his birth date... what are you blathering on about? You know I have no choice but to spend every day with you." She added bitterly, "There has not been an option in some time now."

"Miss? What do you mean, miss-oh. No, Christmas. Christ mass. But you raise a good point. I don't want you to have no choice. If you had..."

"If I?" she questioned testily, the room's temperature dropping severely. "Need I remind you that I am the Heiress of the Seas? The one who saved your sorry sack and equally sorry city from financial ruin?"

What makes you think you have the right to talk to me that way!? He screamed in his mind, but the words never left. He bit his lip and let out a vexed, "Hrmph!" He pressed his index and middle fingers to his temples. "Lai-Kuuvalu. For once in your life, try, just try, to consider what someone other than yourself or your mother is going through."

"Why should I? Especially for someone like you?"

"Fine. Fuck it. Forget it. Let's go back to shared silence."

"That is fine by me!"

The day went on, and when it came time to rest, he lay in bed in the darkness of his room and his thoughts. At a loss for options, he picked up his phone and dialed his father.

"Dad?"

"Teddy! Big man, how's it going? Long time no talk!"

"Yeah... eh... I'm sorry about that," Feodor said a bit quietly.

"Are you alright?" asked the man he thought was named Renat.

Feodor's voice kept low. "I... know dad. About you. Your secret."

"My secret? What are you talking about?"

"Lai-Orani."

There was a silence shared between them. It, with the darkness, was suffocating, and for a brief moment Feodor entertained the thought of sweet release from his troubles by the kiss of nonexistence.

"How did you find out?"

"It's a long story. More importantly, I have a mer—

Posidni… living with me currently."

"What… what are you doing with one living with you? That's a terrible idea. Throw them out," suggested his father in a rushed voice.

"I can't throw her out. She's… a royal. The princess."

Renat screamed through the phone, "FEODOR! FEODOR WHAT IS WRONG WITH YOU!" which prompted Feodor to hold the phone away from his ear. He slowly brought it back over.

"I've been wondering the same thing. Anyway, what do you give a princess for a gift?"

"If you're looking to get rid of her, a one-way trip to the ocean is the smartest gift to give."

"No," he said quickly. He cleared his throat, and repeated again, more calmly, "No. It wouldn't be beneficial to anyone if I got rid of her in any form or fashion."

"What is she even doing on land?"

Feodor wasn't sure if he was at liberty to share that with his father, so he didn't. "Back to the original topic, dad. What do I give her as a gift?"

"… sea blossoms, carved stone with writing on it… those… are good picks. But why are you…"

"She hates me currently. I need to fix it."

"Hoo boy. No, Feodor, if the Queen or her kin hate you, there is nothing you can do about it, and it's best to throw them back in the ocean where you found them."

"That's not an option."

"Is she forcing you to keep her on land?" Renat asked incredulously. Feodor knew he couldn't tell his father the truth.

What was the truth, anyway?

It was that if she went back, humanity was doomed, right? Wasn't that it?

"Thanks for your concern. I love you, dad. We'll talk again

soon." Before Renat could get another word in, the call was ended. Feodor dropped his phone on the bed next to him, and then turned to lay on his side so his back was to it. He curled up a little, hoping his dreams would release him from the confusion of the day.

Despite his yearning to stop thinking of her, he found himself spending his free time looking up stone carving services. Sea blossoms sounded like something made up, so a carved stone seemed a much more likely gift. A thought dawned on him, some two days later, and so he sprung it on her. "Hey, Lai-Kuuvalu, what is the Posidni writing system like?"

"We don't have one."

"... what," he said, staring. "Your ancestors came here from outer space, and you don't have a writing system?"

"Your ancestors as well, and that's correct."

"Shit... you're kidding me," he said, sagging.

"I am not kidding or joking or whatever term you wish to use."

He messed his own hair in frustration. "Augh... thanks... for telling me..."

The next day was Christmas Eve. He slept in... or... tried to. A low knock came to his bedroom door. He opened it to find Lai-Kuuvalu on the floor, looking up at him. "Feodor. It is time for work."

"There's no work today. Christmas and Christmas Eve are holidays."

"Holidays..." She repeated slowly. "... I see."

He looked down at her and sighed. "You should get changed for the day. Here," he lifted her up. It had gotten easier over time. "Hup. What do you say we go out to eat today?"

"Why?"

"To celebrate."

"To... celebrate what?"

"It's Christmas, okay, to just celebrate that."

"I do not partake in these Christmas celebrations. I—" she began, staring at him levelly.

Feodor sighed. "I know, I know. You're the Princess, Heiress to the Seven Seas, She Whose Coldness Knows No Match Save The Royal Queen, holy be her name, glory, glory, glory," he said in an exasperated tone.

"You *can* learn," she said, her lips turning up ever so slightly.

"And you, Miss Princess, can actually smile." Upon hearing Feodor's words, said smile instantly vanished.

"I would never…"

Feodor smiled some himself. "… sure," he acquiesced. "You would never." He shook his head. "Good colors for today are red, white, or green."

"… what strange colors to pick from. I will go with green," she said as she was carried off to the guest room. He set her down on her bed and went to her closet, picking out all of her green dresses. He set them on the bed next to her. "What color shoes will you want?"

"Black will do," Lai-Kuuvalu responded.

He took out her black heels and set them down. "There's a big Christmas party that's held at City Hall every year. Would you come with me, tonight?"

"Do I have a choice?" she asked testily.

He went to her and sat on her bed next to her. He took her hands in his and nodded. "Yes. You have a choice." Feodor gazed into her eyes. "You could stay home; I could take you to the boardwalk… you have options."

Lai-Kuuvalu's cheeks took on a faint blue color as she looked into his eyes in return. "Then…" she said slowly, breath catching. "… I… guess I will attend this party. It will be the first human party I have ever attended, so if you attempt to make a fool of me..."

Feodor shook his head. "I would never." Without thinking, he brought a hand to her cheek, leaned in, and kissed her.
Beautiful symphonies erupted from her chest as they kissed,
and he felt his body yearning to do the same.

When their kiss ended, she whispered, "What... was that
for, Feodor?"

"I'm not sure..." he admitted in a hushed voice. He slowly
placed his forehead on her shoulder and said, "... but it always
feels right, and I hate how right it feels."

"You are attracted to me. It is expected, I am a person to
be desired, coveted, and envious of." Lai-Kuuvalu said with gentle laughter in her voice.

"However expected it is, I don't want to be," Feodor
whined as he sat himself up. "I'm going to head out of the room
so you can get changed." He pushed up off the bed and to his feet.
He took a single step forward...

... and then found his hand caught by hers.

"Wait," she said quietly. "I... am not ready for you to de-
part yet, Teddy. You will wait."

No snarky response came. He went and sat down on the
bed next to her, once more. She leaned up and kissed his cheek,
and then took to getting changed into one of the green dresses.
It was a long green dress that had a dramatic dip in the back and
a sweetheart neckline in the front, sleeveless. She looked stunning, but it was freezing outside. He touched her bare shoulders
and slid his hands down her arms to her hands, where he gently
grasped them. "People will be suspicious of you, tolerating such
cold with so little."

"Let them be in awe of me," she said, tilting her head up
slightly.

In response, he brought her hand to his lips and kissed
her palm. Her hand caught his cheek... and then their lips were
locked once more. He broke the kiss and said, "Breakfast! We

need to go have breakfast." He went to the floor and slipped her black heels onto her feet.

They ate together at the local diner, enjoying breakfast in each other's company. Although she had been feeling off recently, there was something about this atmosphere, about the way they were together, that warmed her to her core. It took all of her effort to not break into song while they were together. After breakfast, he took her to Main Street, and wheeled her down the sidewalk.

"There are so many people out and about," she marveled. "Is this how humans normally are?"

"More are out than normal. It's Christmas Eve, everyone is doing last-minute shopping or enjoying the day together. Well, everyone who celebrates. Not everyone celebrates."

Lai-Kuuvalu furrowed her brow and tilted her head to look up at Feodor. "Is this not a human holiday? Should not all humans celebrate?"

"Posidni aren't all one culture, are they?"

"We are. There are some small groups that have other holidays, but on the whole… ah, I see."

"Yep, we're the same way. Not so different," he said as he wheeled her. The realization was a little unsettling. Not so different? Humans and Posidni? Could that really be the case?

He wheeled her to the park, where there were many stands set up selling a wide variety of goods. "How about we get some things from here?"

"I do not require trinkets," she said with a frown.

"Okay, but you might find something you like. You never know," he said as he began to wheel her through the park. He mentally noted how many people were fine with crossing right in front of her wheelchair like she wasn't even there. It wasn't until she came into his life that he even noticed, no less realized, just how dismissive people were of those who might be differently-abled. Once, he might have even been among them, cluelessly wading through the crowd with abject disregard for someone who tried their best to not run over anyone's toes, literally and metaphorically, on the way to their destination.

Not now. Not today.

"Excuse me," he said loudly as he made his way through the crowd with the wheelchair. He brought her to a stand selling hot cocoa. "Two please, dark chocolate, whipped cream, white chocolate shavings. Thanks." The man behind the counter began to work on their drinks.

"What is this... chocolate?"

"What do you mean "what is chocolate"?" He stared at her. "Haven't you had chocolate before?" When she shook her head, he grinned, and said, "Well, Ariel, I think I've found what will save humanity then."

"... chocolate," she said dubiously.

"Chocolate," he said affirmatively.

"I sincerely doubt a drink, this... chocolate... will warrant saving humanity from my mother's righteous wrath."

With that, Feodor received the drinks. He gave one to Lai-Kuuvalu, and while he paid for the drink, she took a sip. He caught a glimpse of her expression out of the corner of his eye. Raised eyebrows, dilated pupils, slightly parted lips. Oh yeah. *It was a homerun.*

"You were saying?" he asked, leaning towards her and grinning.

"... maybe we should keep some humans to cultivate this chocolate," she mumbled. "Or do trade with the surface for it."

"That's the sort of thinking I like to hear!" He wheeled her over to some tables and took a seat after she was positioned so she was at the table herself. "There are all sorts of foods and drinks from all over the world with interesting tastes and flavors. If you went to New York City, you could probably sample most all of them. Short of that, there's always the internet."

"Let's do that, then," she said, looking over at him. "Feed me the cuisines of the world. Show me more. I want to see and try everything," she said, looking at him.

"Well, if you're pregnant, there's a lot you can't have."

"Besides alcohol?"

"… that's a good point, you don't need alcohol to try every country's cuisines." He sighed, and asked her, "Are you sure you don't know if you're pregnant already?"

"Some women never realize they are with child until they give birth," she countered. "Though how they miss the sound of their child's singing is beyond me."

"Eh? They sing in the womb?"

"Of course they do," she said as she drank her hot cocoa down. "This truly is delicious. A worthy offering to royalty."

"It wasn't… you know what, sure, if it makes you happy," he laughed. "It's just easier to roll with the punches when it comes to you, sometimes."

She made short work of her drink and he threw out both of their cups in the garbage, and then began to wheel her once more. When he did, they saw all sorts of different wares. She stopped him at a stand. It wasn't an official stand, he could tell, by both the terrible off-red paint job on the mismatched plywood and by its worker: a young girl selling flowers made of colored paper mâché and green pipe cleaners.

Lai-Kuuvalu looked at the little girl. "Stop here, Teddy. Girl, why are you working this stand?"

"I want to buy a Christmas gift for Mommy."

"I see. How much does this Christmas gift cost?"

"Twenty dollars."

"And how much is a flower?"

"Two dollars."

"Teddy, you will—"

Feodor already had his wallet out with a twenty and was handing it to the little girl. "Excuse me, young lady, but could you give us ten flowers?"

The small girl held the twenty in her hands and began to bounce up and down with joy. She collected every flower she had and placed them on Lai-Kuuvalu's lap. She took to running down the park with her twenty in her hand, giggling gleefully. Lai-Kuuvalu just watched the little girl run off.

"Cute kid," said Feodor.

"Women should leave such menial work to men. Hopefully this will put her in a better position," said Lai-Kuuvalu. "Teddy, you will bring me to a salon presently."

"Oh? You know what a salon is?"

"Do they not have them on the surface? I desire my hair to be styled in the manner becoming of human women for this... party."

"As you wish," he said deferentially. He brought her down Main Street to a salon that was still open. Upon entry, the woman who owned the shop whistled.

"That's a lot of hair. Do you want a haircut?"

"I want it washed and styled in a manner becoming of a royal... and utilizing these flowers."

"That's just junk, though," said the woman, blinking.

Lai-Kuuvalu glared at the woman, but Feodor's hand found her shoulder. She calmed down, and Feodor spoke. "These flowers are important to her, and if you are really skilled, you'll manage, won't you?"

"... fine," she said with a sigh. "This will be fifty."

"Payment will be given when she's done," said Feodor. "And not a moment before then."

The woman gave a thumbs up and got to work. By the time she was done, Lai-Kuuvalu's long hair had been properly washed free of its salts, conditioned, and was shiny. Some of her hair had been braided and tied in the back, the tie hidden beneath the flowers – all tied together as a bouquet.

Feodor went around Lai-Kuuvalu a couple of times, admiring the styling done. It was really basic, but he liked how she looked, and she seemed to accept it. He took out a fifty, paid the woman, and took Lai-Kuuvalu out of the salon. "Does it suit me?" the Princess asked as they left.

He smiled down at her. He wasn't sure what came over him, but he leaned in and whispered, "It accentuates everything wonderful about you, my Queen."

19 – One, Two, Three

Not a peep came from her for the rest of their day, until night fell and he brought her to his car. "Time for the party."

"Will it be enjoyable for you, with me unable to stand?"

"It will be, because you'll be with me." *Geeze*, he thought to himself. *What's with all these cheesy one-liners today? Is it the spirit of the season?* He caught a glimpse at her face and saw the blue hue to her cheeks. A rush of red came to his own, and he felt himself invigorated. It was worth it after all.

Again, she fell quiet. He brought her home first. "I'll be just a moment. Let me get changed into a suit."

"A suit?" she asked.

"It'll be just a minute. I'll leave the car off for you so you don't get overheated."

"That is... thoughtful of you," she said unsurely.

He smiled at her, and then rushed inside.

Lai-Kuuvalu took the opportunity to open her clam shell necklace, looking at the holographic display that appeared. She opened her mouth and sang the word, "Call," but did not manage a second word. All that burst forth was heartsong. Her hands started to tremble. "Oh Gods... what is wrong with me?" She let go of her necklace, letting it fall against her chest. She put her hands on her head in despair, and felt the sting of tears coming on. "No... no. I am Princess, I am Heiress, I do not lose my composure, others lose their composure before me!" She looked up and saw her reflection in the mirror of the car. She saw the pearls slowly cascading down her cheeks, hitting the floor and inside of the car with soft *clinks*. She saw the look of desperation on her face, the look of loneliness in her eyes. She felt disgusted with herself, and yet... all she could do was sing and sob as she eagerly awaited Feodor's return.

He went down the stairs, back to his car, wearing a dapper maroon suit to match her green dress when he saw his car was partially iced over. It was cold, but not that cold. "Dammit, why is she angry at me now?" He muttered under his breath. He went to the passenger door and heard the sobbing within. His eyes widened.

She wasn't mad.

He mustered all of his strength and yanked the door open with a loud CRACK as the ice broke. He undid her seatbelt and pulled her to her feet and to his heart. She took her fist and pounded it against his chest, but it didn't hurt. All that he could feel was her pain, and in that moment, he felt like he was drowning in it with her.

Feodor brought one arm around her waist, and the other hand moved to cradle her head. He hunched his shoulders forward and tried his best to hide her face from the outside world. "It's okay," he said softly. "Let it out, Kuuvalu... let it out."

He wasn't sure how long they were there, like that, but it began to snow. Wishes he never thought he could have began to flood his mind. *I never want her to cry like this again. I don't know why she's suffering, but I never want her to suffer like this again. Please, God, grant me the strength to heal her heart.* He wasn't sure if his plea was heard, but she slowly stopped crying.

"What... have you done to me?" she whispered hoarsely. "What have you done to me, Teddy?"

His heart skipped a beat. He was Teddy again, not Feodor. He gave a sad smile as he said, "I could ask you the same thing, Kuuvalu."

"We will... need to part ways soon..."

"Don't think about that right now. Today, tonight, it's Christmas Eve. It's just us and the magic of the holiday."

"Magic...?" she asked, looking up at him with surprisingly soulful eyes. He brought his hand from the back of her head to her cheek.

"Magic," he reaffirmed. "Christmas is a magical time. Tonight, you are going to have a wonderful time. I will make sure of it. Now, madam, your carriage awaits you."

"This... is not a carriage," she said, looking to the car. He brought her face to his once again and softly kissed her lips.

"Tonight, it *is* a carriage."

She looked at it and suggested in a voice low and barely audible, as if scared of its sound, "... a palanquin, carried by the royal guard on giant seahorse back?"

"Yes, and we will ride side by side to our destination." He gently got her back into the car and buckled her seatbelt. He prayed it still worked after her ice job. He went to close to the car door... and noticed she was still looking at him. He smiled at her, closed the door, and went around to the driver's side. He got in, buckled up, and placed his hand on the gearshift. She instantly placed her hand on top of his. He looked to their hands, and then to her.

For tonight... she is mine, and I am hers. Just for tonight, it's safe to pretend, isn't it?

For tonight... he is mine, and I am his. Just for tonight, it is safe to pretend, is it not?

They arrived at City Hall, by the valet parking lot. He got out of his car, came around, and helped her into her wheelchair as per the usual. The valet took the car, and Feodor took Lai-Kuuvalu into the large, ornate building.

After making it through the security checkpoint and wishing the security guards a "happy holidays," the two arrived in the large room that had been repurposed for a ball. There were lights, white lit paper lanterns, plastic snowflakes, sprayed-frost on the window to capture the feeling of the cold further encapsulated by the snow falling outside. There were people standing, drinking, talking... and with the live band playing, people were dancing. Lai-Kuuvalu placed her hands on her mouth as she stared all around.

"This... is nearly magical."

"Nearly? What's it missing?"

"Me being able to stand with you at my side."

"Ariel..." he said, only beginning to realize she was getting caught up in a fantasy of her own. "... we'll make something like that happen tonight."

"How? I can't walk, you never taught me," she frowned.

If I had taught you to walk, you would have run right out of my life, wouldn't you have? ... No. Maybe before, but not now.

"I'm sorry... I'm asking you, for tonight, to trust me. I know I don't deserve that trust... but just for tonight." He went in front of her wheelchair and extended his hand out to her, palm up.

"Just... for tonight..." she repeated slowly, taking his hand and looking up at him.

He pulled her to her feet and whisked her away to the dance floor, helping keeping her up with an arm around her waist. All that time carrying her and bags of salt had paid off – he could maintain this positioning for quite some time. And so, he did. They spun around, dancing to the music, the skirt of her dress billowing and extending outward with each spin.

"Is this... dancing?" she asked him as they went round and round together.

"It is. Do you like it?"

"I like it because it is with you, Teddy," she said.

It was his turn to blush and become a little flustered. Around them, people spoke to one another.

"Is that the mayor?"

"Who's that woman he's with?"

"Is she an escort?"

"She's gorgeous."

"They complement each other rather well, don't they?"

"Perhaps she's his new fling?"

Caught up in the gossip and not wanting to sunder *her* good name, he spoke a little loudly to Lai-Kuuvalu. "Ariel Fisher. Thank you for being in my life."

"Thank you for finding me that day on the beach," she said.

He craned his head back a little, surprised she could even thank another. But then, perhaps it was the magic of the night? He leaned in, and she met him halfway, and their spinning stopped as they shared a kiss on the dance floor. Someone whistled, and another person said something about needing mistletoe. He blushed and broke the kiss. "Ariel, I..."

"... I want to dance more. Can you handle it?"

He blinked a few times, and his brow softened as a smile spread across his face. "Of course. Whatever you wish for tonight is yours."

They never stopped to chat with other people or partake in the food being offered, as it didn't cross their minds. For the rest of the night, they might as well have been alone, dancing on air to ethereal music that had no beginning and no end... until it did.

"Uh, Mayor? The party's over," said one of the security guards.

"Thank you, we'll take our leave." And Feodor got her to her wheelchair, and then back to their car courtesy of the valet attendant. It was dark and still snowing. The snow was sticking to the ground. "Where do you want to go now?"

"The ocean," she said, looking at him, unaware of the smile on her lips.

Feodor stared ahead of him as reality came crashing back

down on him like a tidal wave. "Where else?"

"What do you mean where else?" she asked, with a hint of laughter in her voice. "You said whatever I wished for tonight is mine. I wish to go to the ocean."

"No," he said firmly.

The smile he never turned to see faded. "… it was a lie," she concluded, the car starting to get cold.

They sat in silence as they drove back home, wondering if things could have, should have, gone differently that day. They each retired to their bedrooms, staring at their respective ceilings.

Feodor lifted his phone, went through his contacts, and selected his father. He looked at his contact information, and pressed the call button. Seconds later, he ended the call. When he saw his father calling him back, he sent the call to voicemail and turned off his phone. He curled up in a ball, wishing for sleep.

Lai-Kuuvalu opened her clamshell pendant, looking once again at the holographic display. "Call Lai-Zemforau."

20 – Merry Christmas

The next morning, over breakfast, Feodor rolled over in his head whether he should apologize to Lai-Kuuvalu and if so, how. The thoughts bounced around in his mind, rattling his brain. Should he even apologize?

His body ached.

His head ached.

His heart ached.

He couldn't prove it, but he was sure even his soul ached.

"Kuuvalu, I—"

"I called my mother last night," Lai-Kuuvalu said, looking down at her food.

"You... *what.* Why?" Feodor stared at Lai-Kuuvalu, dropping his fork on the table.

Lai-Kuuvalu tensed, and looked up at him. "What do you mean *why*? You won't let me leave, and I have had enough of the surface. It is time for me to go home and to report to her properly."

"No, it's not! I know for a fact it's not; it hasn't been a year yet!" He stood up from his chair with such urgency, said chair fell over. "Kuuvalu, what have you done!"

"I gave my mother my coordinates. I will be retrieved shortly."

"How shortly is shortly?"

"Within the hour."

Now it was his turn to cry; tears peeked at the edges of his eyes. He quickly went to her and crouched down to one knee before her. He put his hands on hers. "Kuuvalu, but why…"

She took her hands away from him, a disgusted look on her face. "… I did not give you permission to touch me." He flinched back a little, as if she had stung him.

"Why? Why have you done this?"

"You could have come with me. Nothing was stopping you. Last night, we could have gone together to the ocean and never had to have this argument, any argument."

"Everything I know is up here, I've only known you for two months, I'm not going to just go to the ocean and marry you!"

"And yet you expect me to stay up here, have sex with you, help you do your job, and save humanity? To what benefit for myself?"

His mouth opened a little. "… it… really does look like that, doesn't it?" Feodor asked quietly.

"It does not *look* like that, it *is* that."

Getting to his feet, he went and righted the chair he had knocked over. "I'll get the wheelchair ready," he said, his back to her.

"There is no need. I will be carried," she said flatly.

"Is there anything, anything at all, I could do to make you stay?"

"No, Feodor. You made a gamble that I needed you more than you needed me, and you lost. Perhaps my child will learn from your mistakes and not participate in such betting." Lai-Kuuvalu got herself to the floor and began to crawl to the door using her arms.

He watched her crawl, and felt his stomach twist. "I should have taught you to walk," he said as he walked past her to the door.

"You should have done a lot of things," she said, voice full of venom.

Feodor's shoulders went up as he said, "I'm not the only one who needed to change what he did, though." He put his hand on the door to keep her from opening it. "You will hear me out one final time, Kuuvalu."

"Lai-Kuuvalu," she corrected him as she gave him her best death glare.

"No. Kuuvalu." He stood over her, glaring right back at her. "You have been almost consistently cold, demanding, and if I'm downright honest, a complete and utter bitch the whole time you've been here. I don't know what I feel for you, or why I feel for you, but there's definitely contempt mixed in there. Talking to you has been like talking to an alien and just about as warm! You need to get that racist, sexist crap out of your person if you want someone other than your own blood to want to be with you, and Gods so help me, if our child inherits that nonsense you spout, I will *personally* turn you into sushi." He took his hand off the door and opened it for her. "Now you can leave."

"Bold words. I hope you never spend time as a Posidni again. You are clearly not made for the ocean," she said as she helped herself out. He closed the door behind her and fell to his knees, crying.

"Stupid bitch! Stupid fucking bitch! Who the fuck does she think she is!" he cried. "Who does she think she is, coming to land and telling us to prove ourselves! Who does she think she is..." *Who does she think she is, clawing her way into my heart!?* Feodor cried more and curled up. He placed a hand on his chest, feeling within him the song yearning to escape and lacking release courtesy of his truly human form, versus Lai-Kuuvalu's not-true-human-form.

He banged the floor a few times and curled forward so that his head almost touched his knees and screamed out in agony that nobody would hear. "She broke me! What did she do to me, she broke me! I didn't deserve this! I didn't deserve this at all! I deserve better than..." and as he said the words, his mind flashed to last night, to them dancing round and round City Hall, in each other's embrace. He thought of the kisses, of how he couldn't help but think of her constantly. Even in his anger and anguish, he couldn't help but see her face, think of her touch, of those rare moments she spoke gently.

Feodor wasn't sure how long he spent on the floor there, crying. It could have been minutes. It could have been hours. It had been a long, long time since he cried anything remotely like this.

Then he heard it. What he was dying to hear.

A knock on the door.

He swung the door open and looked at the floor in front of him. "Kuuvalu!?"

What he saw were two pairs of legs. He followed them up to see the concerned faces of his parents.

"What... are you doing here?"

"It's Christmas, Teddy. We visit you every year on Christmas, and thought it would be good to meet this girl you've fallen in love with," said Feodor's mother. "Don't worry, your father told me all about her... are you okay?"

Feodor's shoulders dropped and he slowly looked down at his hands. "Love? Is... that what this is?" he asked, feeling hollow.

"Teddy, are you okay?" asked his father.

"No... I don't think I'm going to be okay, either," Feodor responded, sounding as empty inside as he felt.

His parents came inside, closing the door behind them.

21 – The Report

Lai-Kuuvalu found herself in the throne room she had grown up knowing for the first time in months. *I was crazy to think I could be away for a year*, she thought as she swam forward. There was her mother and the men who had should have raised her, the men she called her fathers without response in kind, but who had sired her, who knew? She dipped into a curtsey-bow before her mother, low and reverential. "Mother-Queen, I have returned with my report."

Lai-Zemforau sat on her throne, looking at her daughter with her typical icy look. "Speak."

"Humans are pitiful creatures. They are petty, they seek to start arguments over things they have no control over, and they have a palpable hunger for power. Everything they touch, without guidance, is ultimately destroyed or made useless.

"And yet... and yet. They are a delicate people. They enjoy their emotions to the fullest, but their resolve is brittle. The smallest hint of a slight causes them to crumple. They become irrationally angry at having their beliefs challenged and at the hints of everything they know changing or being something other than they knew it to be.

"For all their faults, for all their delicacy, they are a creative, beautiful people. They can craft things we can't even imagine. They create foods the likes of which we have never sampled. *They are not inherently good, but they can learn.*

"They can learn from *us*," she said, before gesturing to her own chest. "*We* can learn from them."

Lai-Zemforau raised her hand to stop her daughter. "Heiress." She lowered her hand, the words pointed. "We can see already that you have learned much from them, and that there is much *unlearning* you will have to undergo." Lai-Kuuvalu opened her mouth to speak, but shut it promptly. "These humans and their toxic mannerisms have contaminated you with emotions unbecoming a princess. We will *personally* train you once more, and if there is any hope left for you, you will return to how you were previously."

To… how I was previously? To before Feodor? That asshole who broke me? That man who has filled my head with himself?

For the briefest of moments, Lai-Zemforau scrunched her pretty face up in disappointment. "You have something on your mind."

"The human I spent time with. He wronged me."

"He is no human, he is a Posidni… and how surprising, that Lai-Orani's child hurt you, our child. In another time, in another world, you would be siblings and possibly even due to wed." This made Lai-Kuuvalu clench her fists. The Queen raised a slender eyebrow. "Oh? You have feelings about this, too? My, your time away has offered you such freedom to weakness."

"I do not wish to wed him, but I do not wish to be apart from him."

"You will wed him, and you will be with him forever; we have willed it, so it shall be."

Lai-Kuuvalu looked at her hands for a moment. *Like you would be with Lai-Orani, mother?* "… thank you, Mother-Queen."

"And now you thank me? A princess, no less the Heiress, does not deign to give gratitude."

"Yes, Mother-Queen."

"Is there anything else?"

"I may be carrying his child. I would seek to become a recluse until said child reveals itself."

Lai-Zemforau's fins fanned out for an instant, then returned to their relaxed position. "Lai-Orani's grandchild," she whispered in thought, turning her head to the side and bringing a hand to her chin. "... this child, if born, is to be celebrated. They will be a royal, as their parents are. And *you*," she added sharply. "are to be celebrated if you can get a handle on those emotions you have let get a hold of you."

"... yes, Mother-Queen."

"You are dismissed. We begin our training first thing tomorrow."

Lai-Kuuvalu gave her mother another curtsey-bow and swam out of the throne room. She went back to her room for the first time since her arrival back home. She took a seat on her giant clam shell bed and looked at her dresser, with its oversized mirror. It was adorned with seashells, anemones, and fresh sea blossoms of all kinds. She looked at her face in the mirror.

"Is this the person I am meant to be?" she asked the Lai-Kuuvalu in the mirror. "I am meant to be as my mother said? Or am I meant to be some other way than has been?

"Am I just a reflection of my mother's dreams and hard work, or am I something else?" She gulped and asked, "Something... more?

"Is there more to me than I let myself realize? Or am I really just an emotionless Princess? But if I were, where have these feelings come from? They bubble up to the surface and come crashing in my face, breaking the image I have of myself, leaving in their wake confusion I cannot contain.

"If he were here, I would blame him. Feodor. He is the source of..." And she sang her heartsong, unable to help herself, just from thinking of him. A few pearls escaped her eyes, and she grew angry at the woman looking back at her. "How weak are you, to fall for some man who used you! It is time to let go of his image, set him free to the ether..." She closed her eyes and imagined herself letting him go, putting her arms out to release him. She saw him, falling into the depths of her memories...

and he grabbed both of her hands before he could fade. Her eyes snapped open and she scrambled back on her bed.

"Set me free, Feodor! Set me free of whatever magic you have placed on me, whatever curse you have woven with your touch! You will set me free!" She yelled, but all she heard in return was the quiet of the ocean. Her room began to grow colder, mirror growing ice. "Whatever you have done to me, I will undo! I will not rest until you have let me go! I will not be held as your captive, not in my own home!"

She slowly moved to hold herself, sitting on her bed. "Set me free, you monster. Set me free." Her eyelids grew heavy as the drama of the last two months began to weigh on her. "... you will... set me free."

22 – Out of Control

The months that followed were slow and painful. Each day was spent with increasing longing and denial of feelings. *I would never feel that way about anybody*, they both reasoned in the beginning.

Feodor, through the guidance and gentle care of his parents, learned what he felt was indeed love coupled with fear. He could not get her out of his mind, and he even took time to imagine what her smile and laughter must have looked and sounded like. He wondered what a happily ever after would look like with this woman, and with each passing day, began to believe it could come true.

Lai-Kuuvalu, through the tender hand and fierce rule of her mother, learned what she felt was irrelevant; it was weakness that was holding her back. Still, she could not get him out of her mind. She dreamt often of their child that was on the way, and of singing their heartsong to their baby who was on the way to teach her to sing. She imagined him sitting at her side when she became Queen, and of the future they could share.

Their parents could both see in their children's eyes the love that stirred in their hearts for the one they thought they could never have again. And try as they might, each through their own methods, they could not shake this person from their hearts.

It was April when Feodor was sitting with his parents, both of them regularly visiting him after work now. He was watching television with them, some movie that he couldn't focus on. A comedy of sorts with a vague romantic undercurrent, but even its lacking plot made him long for the woman who had left beneath the waves all that time ago. For his part, Feodor looked the same.

That couldn't be said of Lai-Kuuvalu.

She had grown larger and lovelier, glowing with the beauty that only pregnancy could bring. Lai-Kuuvalu swam to the throne room today and curtsey-bowed to her mother, as was customary. "You called for me, Mother-Queen?"

"With each passing day, you grow more pregnant, Lai-Kuuvalu. Soon, your child will be gracing us with her presence. We look forward to the day."

"Yes, Mother-Queen."

"You are wondering why I have called for you, surely." Lai-Zemforau stared down her daughter with a typical icy glare. "Especially as your training is going well." She paused for a moment. "I have considered your report in full."

Lai-Kuuvalu's breath caught.

Please… please, please…

"I will spare huma—"

Just as she spoke, their pendants snapped open and their holographic displays came into view, as did that of the Queen's husbands, and every display in the ocean fuzzed, preparing to receive a transmission.

On the surface, every cellphone and television displayed static simultaneously, as well. "What the Hell?" asked Feodor, staring at his screen.

"Maybe it's an EMP?" suggested Feodor's mother. Then the screen displayed a face. "Or not!"

The dark blue face was round and small with large icy eyes with very large pupils, a wide nose with a flat bridge, and full, lovely lips. She had long black hair and bangs. On her cheek was the symbol of Neptune.

"Oh no, it's Lai-Zemforau!" said Feodor's mother.

"No… that's not her. This is worse," said Renat.

"Worse?"

The woman on the screen sang in a language familiar to Feodor, but it was truly transcendental. Even listening to it was like ascending to another plane of existence. As she sang, text appeared on the screen.

PEOPLE OF EARTH. WE HAVE HEARD THE CRIES COMING FROM YOUR SEAS. WE HAVE COUNTED THE DEAD. WE HAVE SEEN THE GRAVEYARDS MANKIND HAS CREATED. I AM THE QUEEN OF THE PLANET NEPTUNE, LAI-ETAIM. EFFECTIVE IMMEDIATELY, ALL POSIDNI AND POSIDNI-ADJACENT PEOPLES ARE REQUIRED TO RETURN TO THE SEAS. ALL THOSE WHO ARE FOUND ON LAND ARE TO BE TREATED AS HUMANS AND BE THOROUGHLY RE-EDUCATED AND SUBJECTED TO THE RULE OF THE UWAN MATRIARCH TSYNSHRI THYSSAHNU.

The image of the blue-skinned woman faded, and gave way to the vaguely insectoid gray-skinned face of a woman with golden, almond-shaped, bug-like eyes. She spoke in accented English with two sets of vocal cords. The text continued.

"Thank you for the introduction, your highness. People of earth, we will be arriving to your planet in the next week. Our rule will be fair and just; we will institute laws that benefit all of the planet, rather than just mankind, and we will personally be seeing to the cleansing of the dead zones humanity has created. We will right mankind's wrongs and teach them how to live in a way that will keep the people of the seas safe and healthy. We have already located several strategic locations to place our industrial cleaners, they will be placed within the month of our arrival.

"Thank you for welcoming us to be the caretakers of your planet, and we look forward to learning about and working with you all. Please remain calm and prepare for our arrival accordingly. This transmission will play again."

The transmission then began to play once more, as indicated.

Feodor stared at his parents.

Lai-Kuuvalu stared at her mother.

"Mother-Queen..."

"... our ancestor-cousins have spoken. This is beyond my control now, Lai-Kuuvalu."

"Dad, what the Hell was that!"

"That was Lai-Etaim, the Queen of Neptune... the one person that Lai-Zemforau can't say no to."

"What! What do we do!?"

"I don't know... your mother and I are going to have to go into hiding, far from the shores..."

"And what about me!?"

Renat looked at Feodor. "You... are free to do whatever your heart desires. You can hide with us. You can go get the girl. Whatever you pick, your life isn't going to be easy."

"Your father's right, but we support you."

"Mom... Dad..." Feodor sobbed and hugged his parents.

"What does this mean for us, Mother-Queen?"

Sounding vaguely vexed, Lai-Zemforau said, "It means more disgruntled citizens to rule over. Expect trouble; no matter where they place these industrial cleaners, it will sound trouble for us."

"What should I do?"

"Be patient. All will become clear soon enough."

23 – Clarity

The resulting month was nothing short of a chaotic mess for planet earth. A not-insignificant number of people were recorded going to the beaches and returning to the ocean, turning into Posidni, Cephaloi, and Kfalli. There were humongous machines the stuff of which could only be dreamed of by Studio Ghibli that reached deep into the sea, placed at the points that would best service the residents of the ocean... or so they were told.

Feodor had made his decision. He got his affairs in order and, one weekday morning, came into the office and went right to Leila's desk. "We need to talk. You deserve to know..."

"... that you're one of those sea-creatures too? I figured that was the case, since Ariel was definitely one. I was just missing that piece of information, that they really existed. I knew Ariel was a fake name, but not why she had one. So, who was she?"

"The Princess of the Posidni, Heiress to the Seven Seas, daughter of the Queen Lai-Zemforau."

Leila sighed and pushed herself back in her chair. "The oceans are truly mysterious places. To think, they've gone without being noticed for so long. I'll be praying for guidance on this." She sighed again, and looked up at Feodor. "You fell in love with a princess. How do you plan on squaring up to royalty?"

"It turns out my father was a Posidni as well, Lai-Orani, and that I inherited the royal gene or however it works."

Leila responded flatly, "You don't show it."

"Thanks," he said sarcastically.

"You're going to have to work on that if you want to impress her parents."

With a laugh to his words, "Why would I need to impress them?"

Leila crossed her arms, looking up at Feodor. "Do you really think a Queen and King would just let their daughter marry anybody?"

"I said nothing about marriage!"

"What are you scared of? You love her, don't you?"

Feodor blushed and grumbled. "Well, look: this is me letting you know that I won't be coming back to the office, possibly ever. I'm going to be moving to the ocean."

"I'll pray for your safety."

"No offense, but I don't think Big G gives a shit about me."

"Who said I was praying to *Him*?" Leila responded coyly. "Anyway. Safe travels, Mayor."

The day came too soon for Feodor to feel comfortable. He was out on a boat with Jim – had been for hours – staring down at the ocean. "Is this really the right thing to do?" he asked his former teacher.

"It's a little late for hesitance, but if you want, I can turn this boat around, and—"

"No, no." Feodor sighed. "Damn it. Damn it all." He was wearing nothing but a pair of swim trunks as he stared off the edge of the small boat. "What am I supposed to do?"

"You're going to go down there; you're going to swim for a long time; you're going to find the royal palace; and you're going to tell Lai-Kuuvalu how you feel. Then, you'll figure it out from there."

"Getting into a relationship with Carlotta was so much easier, and somehow, so much worse," said Feodor, resting his hands on the boat's side rim. "No, I don't want to go back to Carlotta. Just… thinking out loud."

Jim drove the boat still and asked, "What do you see in Lai-Kuuvalu, that makes your heart race?"

"Augh... I don't know! I don't know. She's stubborn, aggressive, and completely alien to me."

"What I heard was determined, assertive, and unique," responded Jim. "Which are all perfectly good traits to find attractive in a partner."

Feodor thought back to the surprising gentleness that Lai-Kuuvalu had expressed when she touched him, the way she looked at him sometimes when she thought he wasn't paying any attention. His heart went aflutter. "Yeah... I guess," he conceded.

"Now, what does she see in you?"

"Fuck... I hope she sees something good in me. Otherwise, this will all be for nothing."

"It'll be a learning experience at the very least?"

"Jim, I'm not a kid anymore, I'm too old for learning experiences when it comes to relationships."

"Love is a learning experience, Teddy, and it doesn't care how old you are." The boat slowed to a stop. "This is as far as this girl will go. The water will be a bit cold for you, but you'll adjust to it."

The two men shared a brief hug, and then Feodor sat on the edge of the boat. Jim pressed his rose-insignia ring to Feodor's cheek, revealing the symbol of Neptune there, and after a few moments, Feodor changed into his posidni form, doing away with his swim trunks. "See you on the flip side, Jim."

"See you around, Teddy."

Feodor threw himself backwards into the water and shouted in surprise at how cold the water was, only to gag on how nasty and polluted it tasted and smelled to him. "Fuck... we really messed up," he said. Or he TRIED to say. The words came out as bubbles. "Ah shit," he bubbled out. He swam in the direction Jim had indicated for him to go.

The swim was slow, laborious, and tiring. As natural as it felt to move and swim in this form, he wasn't used to it, courtesy of an easy, non-athletic lifestyle. *Damn my not even bothering to lift weights. I could have really used some weight-lifting exercises.* He thought back to carrying Lai-Kuuvalu and broke out into heartsong. *She really has imprinted on my heart, hasn't she, that crafty Posidni woman.*

Why am I going after her, anyway? Is it really love? But I don't want to marry her. I just want to spend the rest of my life with her, with each of us driving the other insane. He blinked as the realization hit him. That, for some, was as good as marriage. *I **do** love her… oh God help me, I'm in love.*

24 – Just Keep Swimming

Feodor continued on for a day and found himself near-starving and exhausted... and terrified. He knew there were sharks in these waters and other creatures that might want to take a bite out of him. Just when he thought he couldn't swim anymore, hope – he found another Posidni. He swam to them at full speed until he was in front of them.

It was a man with a pearlescent white tail and nacre-blue skin. He had on his cheek the same trident symbol Feodor did. A wave of relief overcame Feodor, until he tried to speak and more bubbles came up.

The man gave him a puzzled look and pointed to his own chest, singing through his chest to speak. Of course, Feodor didn't know the Posidni language, so this didn't help too much. Feodor tried to speak muffled English through his chest instead. "Do you know which way to the palace?"

"Eugh... making me talk a disgusting surface-language... the palace is in that direction, another day or two, can't miss it." The man said coldly. Had Feodor not spent those months with Lai-Kuuvalu, he might have shrunk beneath his gaze; instead, he marveled at the fact that the sea was indeed abundant in many things: salt, water, fish, and, apparently, assholes.

He swam until the water began to get darker, and then continued on. That is to say, he recognized it got darker, but the change in light didn't ultimately affect his vision. He was surprised how well he could actually see. Eventually, when he felt his flipper ready to give out, he came upon a sprawling underwater metropolis. There were loads of spherical homes, some stacked on one another, others spun 'round a large architectural weight-bearing beam of some kind. He saw Posidni of all sorts swimming about, some side-by-side, others in strange close vertical groups that made him think of remora on top of remora.

The light began to leave Feodor's eyes as he went limp. He heard singing, but he wasn't sure whose it was. Everything went dark. At some point, he heard it, what he had longed to hear in his heart all this time: Lai-Kuuvalu's heart song. He began to weakly sing along with it, scared to open his eyes. But he still willed himself to.

And there she was, before him.

"Kuuvalu?"

"Silence. You must recover," she said to him, all the warmth of her song nowhere near her words.

He looked around blearily, seeing he was in an all-white room with many giant clamshell beds and holographic displays. It was at this point he realized he was hooked up to some kind of intravenous line. "I'm so tired… and so hungry."

"Yes, that is what happens when you swim with as weak a body as yours."

"You didn't think my body was weak in bed," Feodor responded with a tired smirk.

Lai-Kuuvalu's cheeks flushed red and her fins fanned out. She whispered, "Keep that sort of talk to yourself, male."

He looked from her face to her chest, and from her chest to her growing stomach. He lifted a hand up. "You're… beautiful," he whispered. The light went from his eyes as he fell unconscious once more, hand landing next to him.

"Fool," she muttered in the Posidni language. She looked left, then right. Spotting nobody with them, she swam closer and took his hand, resuming her heart song for him.

The next he woke, she wasn't there. He slowly sat up and looked around. "Damn…" *Feels like I got hit by a truck. I guess star-*

vation and exhaustion are close enough, though.

"I see you're finally awake," said a voice with a familiar accent. The voice of a man.

Feodor looked over and saw the man entering through the dilating circular iris door. "Who..." His mind searched, and he realized who he was. "... Lai-Mefore."

"Yours truly, son of Lai-Orani. What brought you to the ocean?"

"Isn't that obvious?"

"She doesn't want anything to do with you."

"Her being here earlier says otherwise."

Lai-Mefore swam closer, stopping before Feodor's bed. "There's no proof of that. But that's neither here nor there..." He touched one of the wires tracking Feodor's heart. "... what matters is that you are going to tell her that you do not desire her."

"Why would I do that?"

"Now, now, *Teddy*. There are many reasons you would do that. Especially..." He bent the wire he touched, making the display tracking his heart show a flat line. "... if I am involved."

"Don't call me Teddy, you're creepy as Hell. Why are you threatening me? You want to bang your own sister that badly?"

He released the wire. "Do I want to have the chance to become king, or otherwise live a life of higher rank and complete luxury for the rest of my days? Hm, yes, I do think that would be nice. There's just one issue." Lai-Mefore leaned in close to Teddy so their faces were mere inches apart. "I..." he whispered. "... do not like to share."

Feodor wasn't sure why, but everything in him screamed, and so, he did. "HELP! HELP!" He called out, both verbally and through his chest.

Lai-Kuuvalu swam into the room and, without a second thought, opened her mouth and let out a high-pitched note right at her brother. He went flying through the water and crashed into a wall, his side turning a deep, sparkling blue as he bruised.

He spoke to Lai-Kuuvalu in the Posidni language. She responded. He gave a weak bow and swam out of what Feodor assumed was either a hospital room or an infirmary.

"You… saved me," he said, staring at Lai-Kuuvalu. "… but why."

Lai-Kuuvalu calmly swam to Feodor and grabbed his chin roughly. "You will be my husband. It is a wife's duty to protect her husband."

"No… no, Kuuvalu, I love you, but I'm not ready to marry you. You have a lot of stuff to work on still. You're practically an automaton that does whatever her mother says."

Lai-Kuuvalu's fins flared at Feodor's words, and she released his chin as if he burned to touch. "An automaton? Really? Whatever my mother says? Have you learned nothing?"

"What… was I supposed to have learned?" he asked cluelessly.

She turned her back to him, unable to hide her contempt. "Do not speak with me."

"You're ridiculous, Lai-Kuuvalu."

"Says the man who came to the ocean unable to speak Posidni, unwilling to learn our culture. May you find happiness in yourself, because you will not find it anywhere else in the ocean." She swam out of the room.

Another Posidni swam into the room at some point later, checked him over, and then unhooked him. He was escorted out of the palace by two royal guards, and the large metal iris door closed shut behind him with a resounding clunk. He looked at his hands and then started swimming in the first direction he chose, away from the palace, away from what he assumed was the capital city, looking to get away from any royal mermaids that he could.

What am I missing? This is all about her shortcomings, isn't it!?

25 – In the Wrong

Feodor's time in the ocean had taught him that fish were not nearly wary enough of him, and he took to eating them to sustain himself. He was grateful that he liked sashimi, or else this would be intolerable. Even so, he couldn't put enough distance between himself and the palace – so he thought.

He came upon a massive, whirring machine that he did his best to steer clear of. It was sleek and metal, of equal parts elegant and horrifying design. Tiered, with many holes that triggered something in his biology he couldn't quite place that made him want to either flee or lose all the fish he had collected in his gut. The sounds it produced were loud and nauseating, screeching and overwhelming the senses. He spotted what looked to be a small settlement near this giant contraption. Despite his better judgement, his curiosity won him over and he swam towards what he assumed to be a village, by its size.

There was a sign as he approached with writing on it in some language he couldn't read. *That…! Kuuvalu, really, lying to me about something so basic!? There's a sign right here in your language!*

As he swam into town, everyone retreated into their respective homes, pulling their children inside and away from him, such that he couldn't even get a glimpse of them. He swam into a building with an open door and a sign over it that he couldn't read. There were people with the lower halves of an octopus, dancing, along with creatures that looked something like squids the size of small children, two tentacles having five smaller, finger-like tentacles extending from them. All of them were flashing colors like a rave, dancing to music that he could barely hear over the machine.

There was a man behind a counter who had the lower half of an octopus as well. He blanched, his whole form turning white and his tentacles curling at their tips. Feodor swam to him, shaking his head rapidly. "No, no, no! Don't alert them to me being here! I'm not like the others, I swear."

"You speak... English," said the man behind the counter uncertainly in English, speaking through his chest.

Feodor nodded. "Yeah, it's my first language... where am I?"

"Crustacean Cove is what its name translates to in English. Why aren't you... you know..."

"I was born and raised on the surface, I'm only half Posidni."

The man nodded. "Half is enough to be royal." It was then that Feodor noticed the strange, cuttlefish-like eyes the man had. "... is this your first time seeing a Cephaloi?"

"Is that what you are?"

"Yes. Cephaloi are the offspring and descendants of the union of Posidni and Kfalli."

Feodor's eyes searched the people dancing and fell onto those strange squid-like creatures once more. "Kfalli... is that one?" he asked, nodding in said creature's direction.

The man nodded. "Yeah, she's one."

It was Feodor's turn to pale. "People like me... had sex with creatures like that?"

The man smiled tensely. "Ah, I see that being on the surface didn't teach you any manners whatsoever."

"No, I mean, you do you, it's just... I can't wrap my head around it."

"You leave the wrapping to those with tentacles – if the palace did that, things would be going so much better in the oceans right about now. Kfalli are living, breathing, thinking people, as are Cephaloi, and we deserve as many rights and as good treatment as anybody else. Of course, tell that to someone who looks like you and..." The man gestured across his neck with his thumb. "... clear off."

"I'd believe it. I personally don't think I could get with a Kfalli. Maybe a Cephaloi... but my heart's already all taken up."

"Oh? Do you have a side piece you were going to swim and meet?"

"Side piece? No." Feodor blinked a few times rapidly.

The man looked confused. "Then what brings you out here?"

"The Princess wants my head, I'm pretty sure..."

"That's rough, buddy. Must have pissed her off pretty good, considering how nice she is for a royal," he said as he pulled out a small bulb. He passed it to Feodor. "Drink. You sound like you need it."

"Nice? Her? Have you MET her?"

The man leaned over the counter, looking up at Feodor. "She tried to get humanity saved. Everyone knows it. She was happy to leave those of us who wanted to be on land, on land. She doesn't kill you for trying to speak to her, even if you're not a miposidni or Posidni. She couldn't be more different from her mother if she tried, despite looking so much like her."

"Your bar is set so low that you have to dig underground to view Kuuvalu as a decent person."

"Lai-Kuuvalu is better than her mother, and that's saying something, since her mother was the one who raised her."

"What about her father?"

"You would think one of the males that her mother mated with would step forward to take Lai-Kuuvalu under their fin, but no; all of them denied being her father and refused to raise her. They are her fathers in title alone. Her mother was the one who did all the rearing on her lonesome."

"Plenty of women are raised by just their mothers and turn out just fine, that's no excuse."

The man shook his head and sighed. "By the standards of the royals, she didn't turn out just fine. Perhaps you are more royal than you give yourself credit for, to judge her so harshly."

Feodor rolled his eyes. "And I suppose you think the Princess needs a gentle man who bows to her every whim and worry?"

"I'm not going to pretend to know what the Princess needs. What the ocean needs is someone by her side who gives two shits about the rest of us. What she deserves is someone who doesn't treat her like shit, though, or that kid she's pregnant with."

"News travels far in the ocean, doesn't it?" Feodor had some of the liquid in his bulb. "Is this... rum?"

"Of COURSE it's rum, who doesn't love rum?" the man asked with a grin. "And you know we all have communication devices, don't you? The clam phones? And holo-screens. Just because we're not out conquering the lands above doesn't mean we lack technology. I'd say we have a limb up on the Posidni, actually, with us having a writing system and all."

"The... Posidni really lack their own?"

"Yeah, can you believe it? They're a post-literate society, but that has its own pitfalls."

"Thanks for all the insight... what's your name?"

"In English, it translates to Sunset-Nine-Cuttle-Moon. On the surface, I went by Sunnin Cut."

"Sunnin, then. Thank you again."

He laughed some. "It gives me goosebumps to hear a royal say thank you, half or not. What's your name?"

"Feodor. And I," he lifted his bulb of rum. "am the sorry sucker who got the Princess pregnant." He drank down the rum all in one go.

Sunnin's jaw dropped and again, all of his colors faded from him, though it didn't last quite so long. He slammed his hands down on the counter, body turning fiery shades of red, yellow, and orange. "You're going to marry her, aren't you?!"

"I love her, but I have no intent to marry her."

"Bwuh... what. Come on."

Feodor stared at Sunnin like he had two heads to go with his eight-some-odd-tentacles. "No "come on," I won't be peer-pressured into marriage. That's a terrible idea."

"What's holding you back from marrying her? Are you scared of commitment?"

"Sunnin, are you a therapist?"

"I was a bartender on the surface for fifteen years, that's pretty damn close. Spill."

"Why are you so upset?"

"I have a royal sitting in my bar, talking to me like I'm just another person, a royal who could potentially shift the entire paradigm, and he won't marry the one woman who could give him that power!"

Feodor set his empty bulb on the counter. "I'm not going to marry her for power. If I marry her, it will be for love."

"And you already love her, you said so!"

"Love isn't enough, she needs to stop being a racist, holier-than-thou sexist. You claim she'd be receptive to that change, but that's not effort I want to put in."

Sunnin took the bulb and put it in a basket of empty bulbs, storing it under the counter. "Do you really think she's going to learn that on her own?"

Feodor turned, his back to Sunnin. "It's not my place to teach her."

"If you won't... who will?"

26 – Suffering Slowly

The next month of pregnancy was slow and almost painful for Lai-Kuuvalu. She spent a lot of time pondering the coral reefs and swimming up to the water's surface to watch the stars at night.

The Princess's days were counted by pain, by love, and by the pain of love. Each day, the image she had of Feodor by her side got farther and farther away from her, no longer just out of reach, but an idealized dream that seemed to fade with the morning light.

Did mother suffer this loneliness? she would wonder as she wandered through the garden's ever-blooming sea blossoms. *No... she would never understand. What is this feeling of betrayal and abandonment? Why does it consume me?*

It was during this month of quiet contemplation and isolation that Lai-Zemforau spent many days instructing her daughter.

"A Princess does not slouch. She does not allow her head to lower, even an inch, to anybody aside from her own mother or the Queen."

"Yes, Mother-Queen."

"A Princess does not merely yes her mother or the Queen either."

"Yes, Mother-Queen."

Lai-Zemforau looked to the guards and dismissed them, along with her husbands. She swam up to her daughter and lifted her chin up to force her to shift her mindset.

It was the first touch Lai-Kuuvalu had experienced in

months.

She began to cry.

Lai-Zemforau withdrew her hand, looking at her daughter's crying face. Lai-Kuuvalu broke into sobs and curled up towards her mother, unable to control herself. "Mother-Queen... Mother-Queen, I..."

The Queen looked left, then right, and, certain they were alone, gently pulled her daughter into a hug. She sang a clip of song to her only daughter and stroked her hair, smoothing it down. She placed her own chin on her daughter's head. "... Kuuvalu," she chided softly. "These emotions are no good for you. Look what they've done to us both."

"I will be better... I will be... please do not get rid of me... you are all I have left..."

"Even if it took the rest of my life to train you properly, I would not get rid of you, my Heiress. When you were in my womb, I sang to you. When you were born, I sang to you. And even now..."

"Even now, you sing to me. I am so grateful you are my mother."

"I know, Kuuvalu. I know. There is no need to say what I already know."

"Feodor... he... is he right, that there is something wrong with me?"

"You are perfect. You may just not be perfect for him. And he may not be perfect for you."

"Can that be true?"

"It is true. If you still wish to be with him, you will have him, though."

"I do not know why, but I wish to, Mother-Queen..."

Lai-Zemforau moved them apart just enough so she could cup her daughter's cheeks. She rubbed them with her thumbs. "Then you will have him, so it is willed, so it shall be."

"What if he never comes back?"

"Then you will do what I did not – you will go and get him yourself. He will not turn you down."

Lai-Kuuvalu sniffled softly, looking up at her mother. "I am so weak..."

"You are not weak. You had one mother and no fathers. You inspire me every day..." She lightly poked her daughter's forehead. "Now, enough of this. We grow tired of these emotions; they are unbecoming to us."

"Yes, Mother-Queen." Lai-Kuuvalu swam backwards, wiping the remaining pearls from her eyes. She dipped into a curtsey-bow. "We look forward to our further training."

"As you should, your emotions have made it necessary to teach you everything all over again."

"Yes, Mother-Queen."

"Now, from the top."

"A Princess does not allow others to dictate her life, save her own mother or the Queen."

Just as soon as the day had come, it had passed as a fond memory for Lai-Kuuvalu that she held in her heart. *How could I have forgotten that my mother made that sacrifice for me? That she sang to me and raised me close to her, where other children are raised by their fathers? I pray I may do as good a job as she.*

Even with all that in mind, she longed for Feodor. She longed for his face, his touch, the sound of his voice, and the little ways that he tended to surprise her. He spoke to her coldly, but perhaps, she considered, there was weight to his words.

Are we royals truly racist? Or are we superior, as Mother-Queen has taught me?

Are we a sexist people? Or are women the superior gender, as Mother-Queen has taught me?

Are we a society marked by oppression? Or are we marked by the order in this chaotic world we call our home, as Mother-Queen has taught me?

Am I a flawed, broken person who needs fixing? Or am I perfect, as Mother-Queen has taught me?

For all his vices, Feodor has never lied to me. For all her virtues, Mother-Queen has never admitted fault.

Is the piece I'm missing Feodor? Or is the piece I'm missing somewhere hidden inside me?

Lai-Kuuvalu spent this day – a month after Feodor had crossed her path weak, feeble, and before the border of the Sea of Death – talking to her mother in the throne room. "Mother-Queen," she said, dipping into a curtsey-bow.

"Heiress. What brings you willingly to us this day?"

"I have matters we would like to discuss about my future rule."

The Queen sat up a little in her throne, steepling her fingers. "There will be some great time before we relinquish the throne to you... but... very well. What is the first matter you would like to discuss?"

"It's..."

Just then, two royal guards rushed into the throne room. "What is it?"

"There is a royal at the gates requesting an audience with Your Majesty."

"Which royal?"

"They go by the name of Feodor."

Lai-Kuuvalu's eyes widened, and without meaning to, she sung a piece of her heartsong. She looked from the guards to her mother with a momentary pleading look before falling back into a facade of cool collectedness.

"We will grant this Feodor an audience."

The guards gave stiff bows and then swam out of the room. Lai-Kuuvalu watched them leave, but Lai-Zemforau's eyes fell onto her daughter.

"Do not make a fool of the throne for some half-breed. Do you understand me, Heiress?"

Lai-Kuuvalu stared at the iris door, waiting for it to open again...

... not responding to her mother.

27 – Who You Are

Feodor swam into the massive throne room. Even on land, he guesstimated, throne rooms were large and opulent. But he was surprised to note how unadorned the thrones were and the abject lack of jewelry any of the royals before him were adorned in. Nothing save their clamshell pendants.

And there she was. Seeing her again, he could feel his love for her breaking through his heart and filling the room. Being apart from her, he only realized now, before her, was suffocating.

Even with the icy glare she gave him, he wanted nothing more than to embrace her.

"Feodor Neftali Petrov," said the Queen with one set of vocal cords. She continued, now with the rest of her vocal cords, singing in the Posidni language, "Why have you requested this audience with us?"

In halting Posidni, he responded, "I… wish… to be part of Lai-… to be part of the Princess's and my child's life."

"What makes you think we will allow this?"

"I will…" He paused and thought back to this last month in the ocean. The faces of the people he met, posidni or otherwise. He thought to the people suffering under the rule of the royals without any hint of release from their subjugation. He considered the sacrifice he would be making. More than that, he considered that a month was no amount of time to balk at, and if Lai-Kuuvalu had changed at all, it likely occurred in the month they were apart. That a month, while a long time alone, could be even longer when spent with another who is trying to support you being the best person you can be. He inhaled. "I will marry Lai-Kuuvalu."

"Will you?" asked the Queen, the room getting colder and colder until ice began to grow along the pillars and thrones. The three male posidni sitting at their thrones shivered, one of which began to rub their own arms.

Feodor stared with a blank expression at Lai-Zemforau. "Isn't that what you wanted? Isn't that what she wanted?" he asked in English, before switching back to Posidni. "Yes, I will."

"What makes you think we will permit this marriage?"

He looked from Lai-Zemforau to Lai-Kuuvalu with a perplexed expression. Lai-Kuuvalu spoke in English, "She asked what makes you think she will permit this marriage."

"Are you kidding me? Is this some game of chicken?"

Despite the inner-Lai-Kuuvalu screaming to the otherwise, she just couldn't break past the icy barrier that surrounded her. "I do not need you."

Unexpectedly, he found himself relieved. "Good. I don't want you to need me." He swam a little closer to Lai-Kuuvalu. "What I want is for you to want me. Want me in your life. Want me in the baby's life."

Lai-Kuuvalu looked to her mother now, who gave a single nod. She redirected her attention to the man before her. "A man who belittles the way of life that has served the ocean for hundreds of thousands of years?"

Feodor countered, "Has it?"

"What do you know of what has and has not served the ocean?" asked the Queen in Posidni, which Lai-Kuuvalu repeated in English.

"I spent the last month among Cephaloi and Kfalli." As he was about to continue, he noted the Queen's momentary display of displeasure as she wrinkled her nose. "They do not benefit from the rule of the royals. Did you know they aren't permitted to live in the capital? And although they do the majority of the farming and harvesting of fish and kelp, they are allocated less of it than Posidni? How about the fact that even in towns or villages devoid of Posidni, they are required to pay a tithe of fish and kelp to nearby Posidni settlements?"

Lai-Kuuvalu stared at him. "Is this all?"

"Hardly. The placement of the industrial cleaners has been almost exclusively in areas that directly affect Cephaloi and Kfalli, and only them. It goes beyond just sound pollution; it is causing their eggs and children to be born malformed."

"What makes you think we care about what happens to the lesser species?" asked Lai-Zemforau. Then she caught a glimpse of the look on her daughter's face.

Lai-Kuuvalu looked horrified.

She had one hand on her stomach, and her eyes were wide. Her eyebrows were all the way up. Lai-Kuuvalu turned to face her mother. "Mother-Queen, we must…!"

"There is nothing we can do," she said flatly in Posidni. "Those industrial cleaners come from on high."

"Feodor… do you have a good relationship with the Cephaloi and the Kfalli?"

Without a second thought, he responded, "Yes."

"Mother-Queen, I wish to marry Feodor."

"Lai-Kuuvalu, I suggest you meditate upon the wisdom of wedding a tentacle-sympathizer."

"What did she just say? Even if her singing is beautiful, it sounded bitter."

Lai-Kuuvalu ignored him. "I wish to marry Feodor," she repeated once again.

The Queen stared forward with a glare that could kill. She spoke in Posidni, "So it shall be. The Heiress will be in charge of overseeing that this Feodor behaves in a way becoming of a royal and learns our language sufficiently."

"Yes, Mother-Queen."

"And this Feodor will be in charge of making sure our grandchild has a proper upbringing."

Lai-Kuuvalu repeated what her mother said in English for Feodor. Feodor nodded and bowed. "As you will it, Your Highness."

"He knows some proper etiquette after all. You are both dismissed."

"Yes, Mother-Queen."

"Yes, Your Highness."

They both dipped into low signs of service and gratitude, only to swim out of the room together.

"I pray to all the Gods above and below that this union will not be a mistake," said Lai-Zemforau to no one in particular. The room slowly returned to its normal temperature.

Feodor swam after Lai-Kuuvalu. "Kuuvalu. Talk to me."

She led Feodor to a door which irised open for her, then closed. He swam forward and it irised open for him as well, and he swam inside. When he heard the door close behind him, he looked around and realized this must be her bedroom. "What are you expecting me to say?"

He swam to her so they were face-to-face. "Say what's on your mind, say what's in your heart, but for God's sake, say it in English so I can understand you."

"Is this a political marriage, or a marriage for love?"

"It's both. I want to be with you and the baby, but I also can't turn a blind eye to what I've witnessed this last month."

"I would not expect you to," said Lai-Kuuvalu softly.

"I understand if that's beyond you, but—what? You... get it?"

She put up water-quotes. "I get it."

"You really *are* different, aren't you?"

She raised an eyebrow, resting a hand on her stomach. "What's that supposed to mean?"

"... nothing. It wasn't meant as an insult. Far from it. It's a good thing. I'm going to shut up now." Which lasted all of three seconds. "What about you? Is it a political marriage, or for love?"

"First thing about being a royal... we do not love. We have duties and obligations, but when it comes to emotions, we are above them. We do only as strictly necessary."

Feodor placed a hand on his hip, fin ears fanning out. "Yeah, okay, I call bullshit on that."

"There are no calls to be made on it. You are half Posidni by blood, so you must learn to embrace the cold that makes a royal, a royal."

Feodor reached out and took Lai-Kuuvalu's hands with his own, internally damning the webbing on her fingers that prevented them from lacing fingers. "I don't want to embrace the cold of being a royal. I want to bathe in the warmth that is our love."

A sparkling blue tint came to Lai-Kuuvalu's cheeks. "Pretty words for a man who refuses to take part in the culture that's half his own."

"What? Are men supposed to be poets or artists or something?"

"Of course. That's why men name children. They are the gentler parent as well, whereas the mother rules with an iron fist."

"There will be no iron or fists in the upbringing of our child," said Feodor as he brought Lai-Kuuvalu's knuckles to his lips. "Just the gentleness I know you're capable of."

"I am the Princess and the Heiress. I—" And then Feodor released her hand to cup her cheek with a hand. "I..."

"You are more than the Princess and the Heiress. You are

Kuuvalu."

"Teddy..."

"I know plenty of who this Princess and Heiress is, and I know we're leaping into marriage kind of haphazardly, but I would really love to get to know who Kuuvalu is." He slid his hand from her cheek to the back of her head. "I've gotten to meet her here and there, but she's so shy, she barely shows herself to anybody." He closed the distance between them and gently pressed his forehead to hers. "And," he whispered. "I have it on good authority that she is a wonderful woman worthy of all of my love."

"Maybe," Lai-Kuuvalu whispered. "she could let herself show to her husband every now and again, if they were alone."

Feodor smiled. "He might like that."

"She might like that, too."

"Ah, there she is," said Feodor, keeping his voice quiet, as if sharing a secret.

"There who is?"

Feodor smiled more. "The woman I fell in love with." He leaned in and kissed her tenderly.

28 – All Good Things

"Feodor," said Lai-Kuuvalu. "How many times must I tell you to not pick at your food and just eat it?"

"You're going to be a mother, but don't mom me," said Feodor as he picked at the fish he held.

"I am not going to have you teach our child to eat in such a manner. You eat the bones too."

Feodor eyed the partially-eaten fish skeptically. "You know, I know you keep *saying* we can digest it and won't choke, but I can't feasibly imagine myself—"

And Lai-Kuuvalu took the fish and shoved what she could of it into Feodor's mouth. He flailed around and spoke through his chest, "Kuuvalu! Cut it out!"

"Eat the fish!"

He chewed on the bones and grimaced at their taste and the crunching they made. He reluctantly swallowed down the part in his mouth and swatted her hands away, getting the remaining out of his mouth. "Damn it, Kuuvalu! That's going to tear my stomach apart."

"You are a royal, it won't tear your stomach apart. I, however, will tear you apart if you instill this fear of eating bones into our baby."

Feodor sighed. "The things I'm doing for this kid. They better be grateful."

Lai-Kuuvalu smiled a little. "They will be grateful. Not at first, but as they get older, they will be."

"That wonderful smile. Thank you for sharing it with me, Kuuvalu." When she blushed and resumed an icy look, he laughed. "You can't hide it from me. I'm your husband now."

"I will hide from you precisely as much as intended."

"Which is not at all. No secrets, remember?"

Lai-Kuuvalu deflated a little. "I suppose not."

"That's what I thought. And I have no secrets from you, either."

"If you became much more transparent, Teddy, I would be able swim right through you."

Feodor grinned a little. "But that's something you love about me."

Lai-Kuuvalu ignored Feodor and gave her large belly a rub. "Any day now, you will be with us, little one."

"I know what I want to name them already."

"It better not be a human name," said Lai-Kuuvalu. "There are some truly atrocious human names."

"Well, no, it's not a human name. I had to ask around for what the word is, but it translates to Pole Star."

"Lai-Ezasolem... that is a wonderful name."

"Yes. They will be taught some of the Posidni customs, but they will be learning English young. And they will also learn the written language of the Cephaloi and the Kfalli." When he saw Lai-Kuuvalu about to protest, he said, "They will need to be well-rounded." Feodor moved closer to her and got his chest near her stomach, and he sang their heartsong to her. He could hear with his acute hearing the soft clips of song from within, as if in response.

Suddenly, Lai-Kuuvalu's stomach moved lower.

"Uh... I guess it's time?"

"Can you carry me?"

"Can I carry you... I'll have you know that nobody can carry you quite so well as I can," said Feodor as he lifted her up. "On account of the fact that I would break some faces if anyone tried to lift my wife."

"You still do not know how to use your sonar. Perhaps that is for the best."

He swam out of the room and off to the infirmary. "We're about to be parents. This is so exciting."

"It is exciting. It is also greatly painful."

"You're pretty calm for someone in pain!"

Lai-Kuuvalu lifted her head slightly. "A Princess does not let on her weaknesses to others." Only to grimace right after saying it.

"Yadda, yadda, a Princess is allowed to scream and cry and throw a fit when in labor. Anyone is. Hell, even I am." Lai-Kuuvalu gave Feodor a look. "Okay, maybe not me, but you get my point."

"My mother... I want my mother to be there, when I give birth."

"Are you sure?"

"Yes... the throne room, please."

"Call her, have her meet us there."

"BRING ME TO THE THRONE ROOM FEODOR."

"Right, to the throne room we go!"

The throne room had been cleared out, save the Queen herself. Not even her husbands attended her currently. She stared at the large holographic display before her. Who else would she be looking at but Lai-Etaim, the Queen of Neptune?

"Lai-Zemforau," spoke the holographic image.

"Yes, Your Majesty."

"We have contacted you to inform you we will be sending an advisor to Earth to guide you in interacting further with the various species of the planet in addendum to the uwan."

"Your Majesty, such an inconvenience is unnecessary. We have everything under control."

"No, you do not. If you had everything under control, there would not be Kfalli and Cephaloi insurrectionists."

"With all due respect, while they exist, they are contained and properly deferential to the throne."

Lai-Etaim stared down Lai-Zemforau. "Contained? Do you believe them posting their demands and plans to the universal network to be contained?"

"We have it under control."

"Perhaps the influence of other species on your kind has been too great for you, but you most certainly do not have it "under control" as you so claim. Nobody who says they have a situation under control ever does.

"You will accept this new advisor and teach them of the ways of the Posidni, and then they will teach you the ways to *properly manage* those of lesser kinds. Is this understood?"

"... yes, Your Majesty."

"At least you take instructions better than your predecessors. If I catch even so much of a whisper of you mistreating the advisor in any form or fashion, I will personally send our militia down there to depose you and your line. Is that clear?"

"As crystal."

"Good."

Just then, Feodor came into the throne room carrying Lai-Kuuvalu, whose condition seemed to be worsening by the minute.

"Enjoy the birth of your grandchild." The transmission ended.

"Mother-Queen... what was... that... about?"

"Do not worry about it. Feodor! Why did you bring her here instead of the infirmary? Are you so incapable as a male that you cannot even—"

"Oh God dammit! I brought her here because she told me to, I wanted to bring her to the infirmary, but damned if you do, damned if you don't, I suppose!"

"Let us go to the infirmary now. Quickly." They began to swim off together to the infirmary. Feodor felt weird, swimming next to Lai-Zemforau. He was rather scared of her, being his mother-in-law and all. That and she could kill him pretty quickly if she decided she'd like to. He hoped the last few months had made him less desirable to kill, but he could never tell with her.

"First grandchild?"

"The only that would matter for now, even if they were not the first. Lai-Mefore has failed this family again and again."

"Would you still say that if it's a boy?" asked Feodor.

Lai-Zemforau responded coolly, "My grandchild is my grandchild, and they will be treated appropriately, regardless of whether or not they are a boy or a girl. All that matters to me is that they are my daughter's children."

"We will… have to… try… again… if…" Lai-Kuuvalu tried speaking between her heavy breaths, but it was labored.

"Shh. Don't think about that right now," said Feodor.

"Worry not about providing an heiress when you yourself have not even stepped up as Queen," said Lai-Zemforau. "All in time, Kuuvalu."

"Mother-Queen… my title…"

"Not now," said Lai-Zemforau. "We are about to experience a momentous event, the birth of your child. Right now, you need all the comfort that can be afforded to you." They arrived in the infirmary where two nurses were waiting. They got Lai-Kuuvalu onto a bed, the room already set up.

"Everything looks good, Princess," said one nurse.

"The baby is in position and looking to exit. It could be any minute now when you meet them," said the other.

"Teddy," Lai-Kuuvalu said, searching for her husband's hand. He grasped it.

"Squeeze as much as you need to, I can take it," said Feodor.

"What if... what if the baby does not like me? What if I am not enough for them?"

Feodor laughed softly. "What are you talking about? They're going to love you so much you won't know what to do with it."

"How can you be so sure?"

"Well," he said, looking to Lai-Zemforau. "I look at you and your mother. You never expressly state it, but it's clear that you love her. Maybe with all of your heart. I think there's enough heart in there to share around."

Lai-Zemforau smoothed down her daughter's hair. "Feodor speaks the truth, Lai-Kuuvalu. There is no greater love than the one you feel from your child. Even if you cannot feel it immediately, that love will be there as they look to you for everything, just as you once had."

"What if I do not feel love for my baby right away?" Lai-Kuuvalu panicked.

"The love can come later, or it may never come," said Lai-Zemforau. "We are above love, recall, Princess. It is your duty to provide for your husband and child. Love, no love, that is your duty. You have chosen to bring this child into the world, and it owes you nothing; you owe them the world. It is a lot to handle, but you have us."

"You have us," repeated Feodor. "And if you are truly above love as your mother claims, you don't have to worry, I can love our baby enough for the both of us."

"It hurts so much," said Lai-Kuuvalu.

"That's normal," said the Queen. "The doctor will be here soon."

When the doctor arrived, the formal birth process began. Feodor could only hold his wife's hand and encourage her. Lai-

Zemforau watched, and felt, for the first time, that it might not have been the worst idea for Lai-Kuuvalu to take him as her husband.

The labor was hours long, but at the end of it, a crying baby Posidni was born. "It's a boy," said the doctor as he handed the small child to Feodor. He had darker skin, a tail checkered white-and-black. His eyes were the same blue as his mother's, and he had short curly hair.

Feodor stared at the doctor, bewildered. "Why are you giving me the baby first? Kuuvalu just gave birth!"

"Name him, Teddy," whispered a tired Lai-Kuuvalu.

"Lai-Ezasolem."

"Console him... he's crying..."

Feodor tried rocking his son, and when that failed, he realized what he needed to do. He began to sing his heartsong to his son, who only calmed some at the song. Lai-Kuuvalu joined in, their heartsongs in perfect unison and harmony. Lai-Ezasolem not only completely calmed down, but squeaked some clips of the heartsong as he tried to learn it from his parents.

Lai-Zemforau swam back slowly, and then out of the room, the only hint that she had been there a single pearl where she had been.

"See, Kuuvalu? He loves you."

"I... I love him, too... may I hold him?"

"Of course." Feodor passed over Lai-Ezasolem who curled up on his mother's chest, listening to her heartsong. "You two look perfect together."

"We are perfect together. The three of us," said Lai-Kuuvalu. The nurses and doctor took their exits at hearing that, leaving the infirmary save the small family.

"Feodor... there is something I need to tell you. Something I should have told you a long time ago. Something that you deserve to hear, for everything that I have put you through, for all your headache and heartache."

Feodor smiled. He had a feeling, but he asked anyway, "What's that?"

"I love you."

www.ingramcontent.com/pod-product-compliance
Lightning Source LLC
Chambersburg PA
CBHW060827120626
46557CB00001B/396